CW00818807

THE DOLL

Francis Durbridge

WILLIAMS & WHITING

Applications for performance or other rights should be made
to The Agency, 24 Pottery Lane, London W11 4LZ.

Cover design by Timo Schroeder

9781912582891

Williams & Whiting (Publishers)

15 Chestnut Grove, Hurstpierpoint,

West Sussex, BN6 9SS

Titles by Francis Durbridge published by Williams & Whiting

Murder At The Weekend – the rediscovered newspaper serials
and short stories

Also published by Williams & Whiting:
Francis Durbridge : The Complete Guide
By Melvyn Barnes

INTRODUCTION

Francis Durbridge (1912-98) was a prominent writer of mystery thrillers for BBC radio from the 1930s to the 1960s. As early as 1938 he found the niche in which he was to establish his name, when his radio serial *Send for Paul Temple* attracted so much fan mail that it led to a succession of Paul Temple serials for the next thirty years. It was no surprise, therefore, that while continuing to write for radio Durbridge also carved a parallel reputation for himself in the newer medium of television. And he began by creating a landmark, with the distinction of writing the first thriller serial on UK television - *The Broken Horseshoe* (1952).

In a published interview (*Radio Times*, 21 October 1971) Durbridge said: "Twenty years ago in the United States, a producer told me that I was wasting my time by not going into television. So that's what I did – I tried to build up a reputation with serials, since I'd vowed never to write a Paul Temple episode for television." So *The Broken Horseshoe* was a true UK television first, a thriller that was a genuine serial, defined as one story continuing over several episodes, and in the light of this C.A. Lejeune enthusiastically reviewed it in her *Observer* column (23 March 1952) by writing: "It will be interesting to see how Mr. Durbridge manages his 're-capping' from week to week, for *The Broken Horseshoe* is a true serial and not a series of associated adventures with a beginning, middle and end. The skill with which such a programme can arrange for new viewers to start viewing here, without boring old viewers or wasting time, will achieve much to do with the serial's success. But if it goes on as well as it has begun, I don't intend to miss a Saturday." In fact Durbridge had already been doing this for over ten years on the radio!

But that was just the beginning of Durbridge's successful television career, whereas *The Doll* came toward the end. Viewers had been enthralled for twenty-three years by the consistently gripping plots that had made Durbridge the pre-eminent exponent of the thriller serial on UK television. He was the master of the twist and turn, the creator of tortuous trails devised to lure his protagonists into webs spun by killers who remain concealed until the final episodes. In addition to craftsmanlike plotting skills, he embodied the "Britishness" factor that distinguished his thrillers from the numerous American television imports that relied upon "sock-in-the jaw" action rather than sophistication.

Great credit for this success must be accorded not only to Durbridge but to his regular producer/director Alan Bromly, who for many years was the guru for Durbridge television serials – just as Martyn C. Webster had been for his radio serials. The Durbridge/Bromly television partnership began impressively with *Portrait of Alison* in 1955, and they cemented their relationship by consistently teasing viewers with the many Durbridge elements that became so familiar – numerous red herrings, cliff-hanger endings to each episode, and the certainty that none of the characters should be believed whatever they might say. In total Alan Bromly was producer/director of eleven Durbridge television serials until 1966 (*Bat out of Hell*), and afterwards was the producer of the first Paul Temple television series in 1969 featuring Francis Matthews (but this was not written by Durbridge, nor directed by Bromly).

The Doll was Durbridge's sixteenth television serial, shown in three fifty-five minute episodes from 25 November to 9 December 1975, although it could legitimately be counted as his eighteenth because *The World of Tim Frazer* (1960/61) consisted of three interlinked serials of six episodes each. The producer of *The Doll* was Bill Sellars, the director was David Askey, and it was repeated from 19 September to 3 October 1976.

For those who wish to view it today, it has been marketed on DVDs by BBC/Pidax in 2013 under the German title *Die Puppe*, containing the English and the German (dubbed) versions; and later included in the DVD set *Francis Durbridge Presents Volume 2*, BBC/Madman, 2016. And the title of the set *Francis Durbridge Presents* is significant in itself, defining a crucial aspect of Durbridge's television career – because his success on the small screen was monumental, with the result that for all his serials from 1960 (beginning with *The World of Tim Frazer*) the BBC gave him the unprecedented accolade of the "Francis Durbridge Presents" screen credit before the title sequence of each episode.

In spite of his Britishness, or perhaps because of it, Francis Durbridge built an enviable reputation in Europe. His radio serials were broadcast in various countries from the late 1930s, in translation and using their own actors; and on television beginning with *The Other Man* (1959 in Germany as *Der Andere*) there was a long sequence of European television versions that attracted a huge body of viewers. So addictive was Francis Durbridge on both radio and television in Germany that commentators defined his serials as *straßenfeger* (street sweepers), because so many people stayed at home to listen to them on the radio or watch them on television.

The Italian television version of *The Doll* was *Dimenticare Lisa* (9 – 23 October 1976, three episodes), translated by Franca Cancogni and directed by Salvatore Nocita; while in Germany the UK production was shown, dubbed, as *Die Puppe* (4 – 5 June 1982, two episodes).

Francis Durbridge always maintained that he was a playwright rather than a novelist, but as with many of his radio and television serials *The Doll* was novelised (Hodder & Stoughton, August 1982). This book appeared in Germany as *Die Puppe*, in Italy as *La bambola sull'acqua*, in Holland as *Het verdwenen portret*, in Spain as *La muñeca*, in Norway as *Dukken*, and in Poland as *Jaguar i lalka* – all of which clearly indicated that Durbridge's international appeal continued into the 1980s.

Melvyn Barnes

Author of *Francis Durbridge: The Complete Guide* (Williams & Whiting, 2018)

This book reproduces Francis Durbridge's original script together with the list of characters and actors of the BBC programme on the dates mentioned, but the eventual broadcast might have edited Durbridge's script in respect of scenes, dialogue and character names.

THE DOLL

A serial in three episodes
By FRANCIS DURBRIDGE,
Broadcast on BBC Television
Nov 25th – Dec 9th 1975

CAST:

Peter Matty . . . . John Fraser
Phyllis Du Salle . . . . Anouska Hempel
Claude Matty . . . . Geoffrey Whitehead
Sir Arnold Wyatt . . . . .Cyril Luckham
Max Lerner . . . . Derek Fowlds
Mortimer Brown . . . . .Roger Milner
Mrs Cassidy . . . . .Sheila Keith
Mollie Stafford . . . . Corinna Marlowe
Linda Braithwaite . . . . Sarah Brackett
Mrs Frinton . . . . .Olive Milbourne
Det-Insp Seaton . . . . John Pennington
Policeman . . . . .Rod Beacham
Sarah . . . . .Dolly Landon
Julian Osborne . . . . .William Russell
Det-Insp Lane . . . . .Paul Williamson
Det-Sgt Colford . . . . Roger Gartland
Taxi driver . . . . .Ken Kennedy
Police Sergeant . . . . .Eric Mason
Policeman . . . . John Livesey
Barman . . . . .Linal Haft
Mrs Galloway . . . . Marjorie Hogan
Judy Langham . . . . Jacqueline Stanbury
Receptionist . . . . Alexandra Taylor
First man . . . . .George Lowdell
Second man . . . . Douglas Jones
Det-Insp Holroyd . . . . Ray Callaghan
Policeman . . . . Richard Borthwick

Airport Desk Clerk . . . . Sarah Nash

EPISODE ONE

OPEN TO: A Street in Bloomsbury, London. Day.

PETER MATTY is walking down the street, deep in thought. He is in his late thirties, good looking, well dressed.

An acquaintance passes him and gives a friendly nod of recognition. PETER ignores him – his thoughts being miles away. Then it suddenly dawns on him what has happened, and he half turns and looks apologetically in the direction of the disappearing figure.

A little while later PETER steps off the pavement without thinking. Several drivers hoot their horns at him, and he hurriedly steps back onto the pavement.

PETER gives a small sigh of relief as he stares after the departing cars. He looks carefully this time before crossing the road.

We see now where PETER MATTY is heading for; the headquarters of his publishing company, a small yet impressive building with bow-fronted windows. A van is just drawing away. On the side of the van we see the words: MATTY BOOKS LTD. MATTY PAPERBACKS LTD.

A UNIFORMED MESSENGER comes out of the building and salutes PETER.

UNIFORMED MESSENGER: Good afternoon, Mr Matty.

PETER comes out of his thoughts.

PETER: Oh – good afternoon, George.

Still deep in thought PETER moves on into the building. The UNIFORMED MESSENGER looks quizzically after him, slightly shaking his head. As PETER enters the building, we see the brass plate by the side of the door:

MATTY BOOKS LTD

MATTY PAPERBACKS LTD

CUT TO: MOLLIE STAFFORD's Office. Day.

MOLLIE STAFFORD, PETER's secretary, is on the telephone. She is an attractive, efficient girl, inclined to be excitable at times.

MOLLIE: (*On the phone*) … No, I'm afraid you can't, Mr Matty isn't here at the moment. I'm sorry, I don't know when he'll be in the office … Yes, of course I'm expecting him … I'm sorry, I just don't know … Yes, please do that … Thank you for calling … (*She puts the phone down and picks up another receiver which is on the desk*) Sorry about that, Mr Walters. Look – it's just occurred to me. Mr Matty probably sent your proofs to someone else by mistake … Yes, well – I'm afraid he has been doing some very odd things just recently … Anyway, not to worry, I'll send another set … Yes, of course – leave it with me.

As MOLLIE replaces the receiver and scribbles a note on her pad PETER enters.

MOLLIE: (*Surprised and relieved to see PETER*) Oh, good afternoon, Mr Matty! Am I glad to see you!

PETER: (*Disinterested*) Hello, Mollie. Any messages?

MOLLIE: (*Laughing*) You must be joking! (*She tears several pages off the pad and hands them to PETER*) And your brother's waiting to see you.

PETER stares at MOLLIE.

PETER: Claude?

MOLLIE: Yes. He arrived about half an hour ago.

PETER: But Claude's in Madrid! He's playing there this evening!

MOLLIE: (*Shaking her head*) He's in your office. The concert's been cancelled.

4

CUT TO: PETER MATTY's Office. Day.

A large, book-lined room, furnished more as a study than a conventional office. As PETER enters, we see the back of a tall, distinguished looking man seated in a chair. He has been looking at a magazine. He now turns as he rises from the chair. It is CLAUDE MATTY, PETER's brother.

CLAUDE: Hello, Peter! How are you, dear boy?

PETER: Claude, I thought you were in Madrid! I couldn't believe it when Mollie said you were here.

CLAUDE: The concert was cancelled.

PETER: Oh – why was that?

CLAUDE: The conductor – an Italian called Enrico Muralto – was in some sort of trouble and the poor devil suddenly decided to commit suicide.

PETER: Oh, my God …

CLAUDE: It was a nasty business, I felt terribly sorry for his wife. A sweet little woman.

PETER: Well – I must say, it's nice to see you, Claude. (*Patting CLAUDE's arm*) It really is! And you look fine, in spite of everything.

CLAUDE: (*Looking at PETER*) I'm all right. A little tired perhaps.

PETER: Yes, well – that's not surprising. You work too hard. Where's your next recital?

CLAUDE: San Francisco; but it's not for six weeks, thank goodness!

PETER: Six weeks – that's quite a break.

CLAUDE: Yes, and I'm looking forward to it. I haven't had a holiday – not a real holiday – for years.

PETER: I know you haven't. What are you going to do, pop down to the South of France?

CLAUDE: No, I rather fancy staying in England, for part of the time, at any rate. I thought I might even

5

hibernate on that boat of yours. If that's all right
with you, of course?

PETER: Of course it is! That's a splendid idea.

Pause. CLAUDE is looking at PETER.

CLAUDE: You've lost weight since I saw you last.

PETER: Have I?

CLAUDE: Yes …

PETER: I … don't think so. Well – perhaps a little.

CLAUDE: (*Still looking at PETER*) Peter, I'm worried. Very
worried.

PETER: Worried? About what?

CLAUDE: (*Quietly*) About you.

PETER: Me? Good heavens, Claude! Why are you worried
about me?

CLAUDE: Don't you know why?

PETER: No.

CLAUDE: Then I'll tell you. I've written you four letters in
the past fortnight and you haven't replied to any of
them. Then when I telephoned you last Sunday
morning you sounded vague and confused, almost
unfriendly.

PETER: Unfriendly? My dear chap, you're talking
nonsense!

CLAUDE: (*Shaking his head*) Quite apart from my feelings,
during the past ten days I must have received at
least a dozen letters from people. Friends of ours.
They all tell exactly the same story. They say
you're bad-tempered, morose, and quite obviously
worried to death about something.

PETER: (*Not looking at CLAUDE*) That's ridiculous! Just
idle gossip! There's absolutely nothing the matter
with me.

*MOLLIE enters with a handful of documents and several
manuscripts. She puts them down on PETER's desk and after*

a quick glance at CLAUDE goes out. PETER notices the look she has given his brother.

PETER: Has Mollie been saying things about me?

CLAUDE: (*Lying*) No, of course not. Why should she? You've just told me there's nothing the matter with you.

PETER: (*Relenting somewhat*) I – I wondered, that's all. I wondered if she'd been complaining about … Well, to be honest, she's been having a tough time just recently. I've been away from the office quite a bit and consequently … things have rather … piled up on her …

CLAUDE: Why have you been away from the office? Have you been ill?

PETER: No. I've told you. I'm perfectly all right. There's nothing for you, or anyone else, to worry about.

Pause.

CLAUDE: Peter, we're going to see a lot of each other during the next couple of weeks. At least, I hope so.

PETER: I hope so too.

CLAUDE: Then what's this all about? I'm going to find out sooner or later, so you might just as well tell me now.

PETER hesitates, not sure whether to confide in his brother or not. He turns, and crossing to the window, stands staring down into the street. CLAUDE watches him, is finally about to say something, then changes his mind.

Long pause.

PETER: You remember when I flew out to Geneva a few weeks ago, to attend your concert?

CLAUDE: Yes.

PETER: Well – I don't suppose you remember what happened on the Monday morning?

CLAUDE: On the Monday morning?

7

PETER: Yes.

CLAUDE: (*Puzzled*) I drove you to the airport.

PETER turns and looks at CLAUDE.

PETER: (*Quietly*) Yes, that's right. You drove me to the airport.

CUT TO: Geneva Airport. Day.

A car drives up and PETER gets out from the passenger seat. CLAUDE gets out from the driver's seat and goes to the boot to take out PETER's suitcase.

A little distance away a taxi driver draws up and PHYLLIS DU SALLE gets out. PHYLLIS is an attractive, well-dressed woman. She hails a porter who takes her two suitcases. PHYLLIS reaches inside the taxi for a book, a magazine, and a gift-wrapped parcel and several other small parcels. She is also carrying her handbag. She drops one of the parcels and the taxi driver picks it up and hands it to her.

PETER idly watches PHYLLIS as CLAUDE brings his suitcase.

PHYLLIS pays the taxi driver, at the same time trying to hold on to her book, magazine, and parcels. As she moves towards the main hall, she drops one of the parcels. She stoops to pick it up and succeeds in dropping her magazine.

PETER, amused, says something to CLAUDE, who smiles. Then PETER moves to PHYLLIS and picks up the magazine, tucking it under PHYLLIS's arm.

PHYLLIS: Oh! Thank you!

PETER: Not at all.

PETER goes back to CLAUDE and they move on into the main hall.

CUT TO: Geneva Airport. Main Hall. Day.

PHYLLIS DU SALLE, clutching her book, parcels, etc is looking at the newspapers on the bookstall. She picks up a

newspaper, intending to buy it. She drops one of her parcels.
As she stoops to pick it up PETER hands it to her.
PHYLLIS: Oh!
PETER: Yes – I'm afraid it's me again! There we are.
PHYLLIS: Thank you very much!
PETER gives a faint smile and picks up a magazine from the
counter.

CUT TO: Inside an aircraft. Day.
Passengers are taking their seats in the first-class section of
the aircraft. PETER moves to a seat unaware that PHYLLIS is
just behind him. He drops the magazine he bought at the
bookstall just as he is in the act of moving into a seat. As he
stoops to retrieve it Phyllis hands it to him. They look at each
other; they both laugh.

CUT TO: Geneva Airport. Day.
The aircraft taking off.

CUT TO: Inside the aircraft. Day.
The aircraft is now in flight. An Air Hostess is serving drinks.
PETER takes the drinks, places one for PHYLLIS. We see now
that she is seated next to him.
PHYLLIS: Thank you. I can do with that.
PETER: Are you nervous of flying?
PHYLLIS: No. Just petrified.
PETER: (*Laughing*) I don't think anyone really likes it.
Pause.
PHYLLIS: Excuse me asking, but – the man who saw you off
              at the airport. Was it Claude Matty, the pianist?
PETER: Yes, it was.
PHYLLIS: I thought so! I thought I recognised him!
PETER: He had a recital last night, in Geneva.
PHYLLIS: Yes, I know. I went to it.

9

PETER: Did you enjoy it?

PHYLLIS: Very much. I think he's fabulous. The first time I
             heard him play was in Washington about seven
             years ago. I thought then he was fabulous, and I
             still think so. Is he a friend of yours?

PETER: He's my brother.

PHYLLIS: (*Taken aback*) Oh. Oh – really?

PETER: Really.

PHYLLIS: (*Faintly   embarrassed*)   Well,   I   think   he's
             absolutely …

PETER: Fabulous?

PHYLLIS: (*Laughing*) Yes.

PETER: I'll tell him so.

PHYLLIS: I'm sure he's used to hearing people say how
             wonderful he is.

PETER: Yes – but he still likes to hear it.

PHYLLIS: (*After a moment*) Are you a musician, Mr …
             Matty?

PETER: Peter Matty. No, I'm a publisher. I publish books.
             (*Indicating the book on PHYLLIS's lap*) As a
             matter of fact, that's one of ours you're reading.

PHYLLIS: Oh!

PETER: I gather you don't like it?

PHYLLIS: (*Laughing*) Not very much. (*Tiny pause*) Do you
             go to many of your brother's concerts?

PETER: Not as many as I'd like to.

PHYLLIS: I imagine he travels a great deal.

PETER: Yes, a great deal. All over the world, in fact.
             (*Pause*) Are you on holiday, Miss – Mrs …?

PHYLLIS: Mrs. Phyllis Du Salle.

PETER: Mrs Du Salle.

PHYLLIS: Yes, I suppose you could call it a holiday. This is
             my first visit to England although curiously
             enough my husband was English. He emigrated to

10

America in 1965. (*PETER registers the "was" but makes no comment*) Norman – my husband – was killed in an accident about six months ago.

PETER: Oh – I'm sorry. (*Tiny pause*) And you've never been to England?

PHYLLIS: No, I haven't. Norman and I used to talk about it. We made plans, on more than one occasion, but somehow … it just never worked out.

PETER: (*Curious*) But – forgive me – your accent …

PHYLLIS: It's very English?

PETER: Yes.

PHYLLIS: (*Laughing*) I know, everyone tells me that. Actually, I was born in Boston. My father was in the Diplomatic Service and we were constantly meeting English people so probably that has something to do with it.

Pause.

PETER: Where are you staying in England?

PHYLLIS: I shall be in London for four or five days and then I'm probably going down to Dor-set. Dor-set, is that right?

PETER: Dorset, yes, that's right.

PHYLLIS: A great friend of my late husband lives at a place called Heatherdown.

PETER: Oh, I know Heatherdown.

PHYLLIS: You do?

PETER: Yes, quite well. I have a boat at Poole Harbour, it's about twelve miles away. Heatherdown's very nice. You'll like it.

PHYLLIS: So I'm told. Perhaps you know Sir Arnold?

PETER: Sir Arnold?

PHYLLIS: Sir Arnold Wyatt.

PETER: No – I don't think so. I don't recall the name.

11

PHYLLIS: He's a lawyer; at least he was. I believe he retired a couple of years ago. (*She opens her handbag and consults a pocket diary*) Forest Gate Manor, Orchard Place, Heatherdown.

PETER shakes his head.

PHYLLIS: We've never met but I've heard so much about him I feel as if we're old friends. (*Tiny pause*) My husband's parents died when he was quite young, and Sir Arnold looked after him for a time. Norman was very fond of him.

PETER: Was your husband a lawyer?

PHYLLIS: No, he was a journalist. He was quite well known in America.

PETER: (*Thoughtfully*) Norman Du Salle. Yes, of course.

PHYLLIS: You probably read about the accident. It was in all the papers.

PETER hesitates, he is about to question PHYLLIS, then changing his mind takes out his wallet and hands her his card.

PETER: If I can help you at all while you're in London, please don't hesitate to give me a ring.

PHYLLIS: That's most kind of you, Mr Matty. I appreciate it. (*She looks at the card, and then smiles at PETER*) I shall be staying at the Connaught.

CUT TO: The Aircraft in flight; about to land at Heathrow.

We hear PETER's voice over the film of the aircraft in flight.

PETER: (*Voice over*) I was pretty busy during the next twenty-four hours, but I must confess I found myself thinking of the flight from Geneva and my meeting with Phyllis Du Salle. In fact, I very nearly called in the Connaught in the hope of seeing her, but at the very last moment I changed my mind. On the Wednesday I'd arranged to take

12

Max Lerner out to lunch – he's an old Fleet Street friend – and he'd just finished doing some research work for me.

CUT TO: A Street in Bloomsbury. Day.
The Headquarters of PETER MATTY's Publishing House.
PETER and MAX LERNER, a young journalist, come out of the building and move to the car which is parked outside. The driver opens the car door and PETER and MAX get in. The car drives off.

CUT TO: Inside the car. Day.
The car is in motion through the London streets.
PETER and MAX LERNER are in the back of the car.

MAX: … I'm glad you're pleased with my work, Peter. But it was a pretty hard slog, I can tell you. Far more difficult than I expected.

PETER: (*Pulling Max's leg*) Yes, I know. And I know the next line, too, Max – you've been grossly underpaid.

MAX: (*Laughing*) Well – you said it! Tell me: how did you get on in Geneva?

PETER: It was a wonderful evening and Claude was delighted with the reception. I must say, he had every reason to be.

MAX: How is your brother?

PETER: He's fine. Working far too hard, as usual. Have you met Claude?

MAX: Yes, I met him several years ago. If I remember rightly, I interviewed him for some magazine or other. I doubt very much whether he remembers.

The car has pulled up at traffic lights. PETER glances idly out of the car window. There is an immediate reaction from him.

13

CUT TO: London Street. Day.

PETER's car is stopped at the traffic lights. PETER and MAX are in the back seat. There is a Mini on PETER's side of the car. PETER is staring at the driver of the Mini in amazement. The driver is PHYLLIS DU SALLE. She is oblivious of PETER's stare, her eyes are on the traffic lights. PETER quickly winds down his window. He calls:

PETER: Dropped any good parcels lately?

PHYLLIS turns, obviously surprised. She laughs, pleased to see Peter.

PHYLLIS: Why – hello!

PETER: How do you like London?

PHYLLIS: I think it's absolutely …

PETER: Fabulous!

PHYLLIS: (*Laughing*) That's right.

A slightly awkward pause. PETER and PHYLLIS are smiling at each other.

PETER: What are you doing tonight?

PHYLLIS hesitates. The traffic lights have changed, and the cars start to move forward.

PHYLLIS: I – I don't know. I haven't thought about it.

PETER: Let's have dinner together. I'll pick you up at eight o'clock.

PETER's car shoots ahead and he calls back.

PETER: Eight o'clock!

PHYLLIS gives a little wave of assent. The Mini turns off at the lights in a different direction to PETER's car.

CUT TO: Inside the car. Day.

The car is moving through London streets. As before, PETER and MAX LERNER are in the back seat.

MAX: (*Grinning*) You bachelors certainly know how to take advantage of traffic.

14

PETER:	Her name's Phyllis Du Salle. I met her on the plane coming back from Geneva.
MAX:	Du Salle?
PETER:	Yes.
MAX:	Any relation to Norman Du Salle?
PETER:	(*Surprised*) Yes, she's his wife. Widow, I should say. Did you know Du Salle?
MAX:	No, not really. I met him once, at a press conference. But we only exchanged half-a-dozen words. I didn't really care for him.
PETER:	I know he was a journalist, but – what did he write, exactly?
MAX:	He was a columnist. A sort of political gossip writer. No, I suppose that's a little unkind, because at one time he made quite a name for himself. (*A moment*) The poor devil was drowned, you know.
PETER:	Drowned?
MAX:	Yes. I was in Paris when the accident happened; the French papers were full of it.
PETER:	What happened exactly?
MAX:	Mrs Du Salle and her husband were on a trip to Europe. They decided to go to Corsica and boarded a ship at Marseilles. Apparently, it was a very rough passage. Heavy seas; the lot. The poor devil just disappeared.
PETER:	What do you mean – disappeared?
MAX:	He fell overboard.
PETER:	Good God!
MAX:	His body was washed up several days later and – Phyllis did you say her name was? – identified it.
PETER:	Poor woman! What a terrible experience.
MAX:	Yes, it was – in more ways than one. (*PETER looks at MAX*) There was a lot of gossip. Talk of

15

suicide. Several of the papers inferred there'd been a quarrel of some kind.

PETER: Had there been a quarrel?

MAX: Yes, I'm afraid so. His wife admitted it at the inquest; fortunately for her they brought in a verdict of accidental death. (*A moment*) Personally, I don't think the row had anything to do with what happened. It was just one of those silly man-and-wife quarrels. If I remember rightly, it was something to do with a doll …

CUT TO: London Street. Day.

PETER's car is moving through London traffic.

PETER: (*Voice over*) I had lunch with Max Lerner and then dropped in on one of our authors. One of our most loquacious authors, I might add. It was very nearly four o'clock when I arrived back at the office.

CUT TO: MOLLIE STAFFORD's Office. Day.

MOLLIE is busy typing when PETER enters. He appears distinctly pleased with life.

PETER: Hello, Mollie!

MOLLIE: There's been a call from New York. They're ringing again at five o'clock.

PETER: Bully for New York!

MOLLIE: The Lazenby contract's arrived, it's on your desk.

PETER: Splendid!

PETER crosses to his office door.

MOLLIE: Oh – and a Mrs Du Salle telephoned.

PETER stops, turns.

PETER: Yes?

MOLLIE:	She says she's very sorry but she can't see you this evening after all.
PETER:	She can't see me?
MOLLIE:	That's right.
PETER:	Is … that all she said?
MOLLIE:	Yes. That's all.
PETER:	Did she ask to speak to me?
MOLLIE:	No. She just left the message.
PETER:	(*A moment, then:*) I see. Thank you, Mollie.

PETER goes into his office.

CUT TO: PETER MATTY's Office. Day.

PETER is attempting to read a manuscript, but it is obvious that his thoughts are on his cancelled dinner date with PHYLLIS DU SALLE. After a little while he throws the manuscript onto the desk and, rising, crosses to the window. He stands staring out into the street.

PETER:	(*Voice over*) I was both disappointed and annoyed that my dinner date with Phyllis Du Salle had been cancelled. And I couldn't help wondering why she'd cancelled it. At one point I thought of telephoning her, then an idea occurred to me. I made up my mind to drop in the Connaught later that evening in the hope of seeing her.

CUT TO: Outside the Connaught Hotel, London. Evening.

A taxi has arrived at the hotel and PETER is paying the driver. As the driver is searching for change, PHYLLIS and a rather over-dressed woman – LINDA BRAITHWAITE – appear on the steps of the hotel.

PETER:	(*Voice over*) I arrived at the hotel at about half-past seven and to my surprise, just as I was paying off the taxi, Phyllis suddenly appeared.

She was obviously saying goodbye to a friend of hers.

PHYLLIS is saying goodbye to her American friend and doesn't immediately notice that PETER is standing on the pavement, quietly watching her. It is LINDA who first becomes aware of the fact that they have an interested spectator.

LINDA: I'll pick you up tomorrow morning, honey, about eleven o'clock.

PHYLLIS: Yes, all right, Linda.

LINDA: (*Noticing PETER*) Are you sure you won't have dinner with me this evening?

PHYLLIS: Absolutely sure! It's very kind of you and I appreciate it, but I simply must have an early night for a change. Truly, darling.

LINDA: (*Aware of PETER approaching*) All right, my dear. If that's what you want. (*Kissing PHYLLIS*) Take care of yourself!

PETER: Good evening …

PHYLLIS: (*Turning; surprised*) Oh! Hello! (*Embarrassed*) Didn't – didn't you get my message?

PETER: Yes, I did. Thank you very much.

PETER smiles at LINDA who immediately smiles back at him.

PHYLLIS: This is a friend of mine. Mrs Braithwaite. Mr … Matty.

LINDA: (*Curious*) Mr Matty.

PETER: Pleased to meet you, Mrs Braithwaite.

There is a faintly awkward silence. LINDA is now looking at PHYLLIS.

LINDA: Well, I guess I'll be making a move. It was a lovely surprise bumping into you, Phyllis. I'm looking forward to tomorrow morning.

PHYLLIS: Me too, Linda.

LINDA: Goodbye, Mr Matty. Nice to have met you.

PETER: (*Looking at Phyllis*) Goodbye, Mrs Braithwaite.
LINDA gives PHYLLIS a friendly little wave and departs.
PHYLLIS: (*Slightly embarrassed; making conversation*) I
            met Linda – Mrs Braithwaite – in Switzerland
            and we became quite friendly. I'd no idea she
            was in London.
PETER: Oh. Oh, I see.
Pause.
PHYLLIS: I'm sorry about tonight, but I've had a frightfully
            busy day and …
PETER: That's all right. Not to worry.
PHYLLIS: I really have had a hectic time and I … thought
            I'd like to have an early night for a change.
PETER: Why not (*Another pause*) How do you like the
            Mini?
PHYLLIS: The Mini? Oh – the car! Very much. I love
            driving.
PETER: Even in London?
PHYLLIS: Yes – even in London.
PETER: My word, you are a glutton for punishment!
An awkward silence.
PHYLLIS: I rented it. The car, I mean.
PETER: (*Still looking at PHYLLIS*) Yes. Yes, I rather
            thought you had.
PHYLLIS: (*A moment, then:*) Well – goodnight, Mr Matty.
PETER: (*Looking at his watch*) Half-past seven. You are
            having an early night! Look – if we can't have
            dinner together, won't you let me buy you a
            drink? (*PHYLLIS is obviously hesitating*) A very
            small drink. You can drink it very quickly.
PHYLLIS suddenly smiles and gives a little nod.

CUT TO: Cocktail Bar: Connaught Hotel, London.
PETER and PHYLLIS are sitting at a corner table.

19

PETER: (*Voice over*) We stayed in the cocktail bar for
              about forty minutes. She was pleasant, quite
              friendly, in fact, in a curious sort of way. But she
              still refused to have dinner with me. It was after
              she'd finished her drink that she started to talk
              about her husband.

PETER: When are you going to Heatherdown?

PHYLLIS: At the weekend. I spoke to Sir Arnold this
              morning. I believe I told you about Sir Arnold
              Wyatt?

PETER: Yes, you did.

PHYLLIS: He sounded awfully nice on the phone, which
              was quite a relief.

PETER: Why a relief?

PHYLLIS: Well – over the years I've heard so much about
              him from my husband, I … suddenly felt nervous
              of meeting him. I don't quite know why. Up to
              now I've been looking forward to it. Anyway,
              I'm sure he's very nice.

PETER: Yes, I'm sure he is. Will you be staying in
              Heatherdown?

PHYLLIS: I … think so. Sir Arnold's invited me down for
              the weekend; but to be truthful I haven't really
              decided whether I shall stay with him or not.
              (*Pause; slight hesitation, then:*) This morning …
              when you were in the car … you had a friend
              with you.

PETER: Yes. Max Lerner. He's a journalist.

PHYLLIS: Max Lerner! That's right! I thought I recognised
              him. I couldn't remember his name.

PETER: (*Surprised*) You know Max?

PHYLLIS: We've met. A long time ago. I met him with my
              husband. He probably doesn't remember.

PETER: (*Somewhat puzzled*) No, I don't think he does.

20

PHYLLIS: (*Quietly; looking at PETER*) What did Mr Lerner tell you?
PETER: (*Faintly surprised by both the question and tone of voice*) Tell me? About what?
PHYLLIS: About my husband; about the accident?
PETER: Oh – he just said he was in Paris when it happened and … he'd read about it.
PHYLLIS: In the French newspapers?
PETER: Yes.
PHYLLIS: (*Still looking at him*) Did he tell you about the quarrel I had with my husband?
PETER: (*A shade embarrassed*) Yes, I think so. I believe he mentioned it.
PHYLLIS: It was a stupid, ridiculous row. It ought never to have happened. It was about a doll that Norman bought just before we left Marseilles.
PETER: A doll?
PHYLLIS: Yes. I know it sounds odd, but my husband was crazy about dolls, he just couldn't resist them – especially if they wore costumes. German dolls, Swiss dolls, French dolls, you name them, he bought them!
PETER: Yes, well – people collect all sorts of things. Believe it or not, I have a friend who collects shoe-horns.
PHYLLIS: Shoe-horns?
PETER: Yes, he's got over two hundred of them. All shapes, all sizes.
PHYLLIS: That is unusual.
PETER: Yes, it is. He still uses his fingers when he puts his shoes on.
PHYLLIS smiles.
A pause.
PETER: You were … telling me about your husband.

21

PHYLLIS: (*A moment, then:*) We'd purchased a Land Rover in Paris and we were taking it from Marseilles to Corsica on the overnight boat. It was a dark, unpleasant night and when we left Marseilles there was quite obviously a storm blowing up. We'd been at sea for about an hour, and I was searching for some seasick tablets when I suddenly realised that I'd forgotten to pack the doll. I told Norman and, to say the least, he was extremely annoyed. Well – one thing led to another and finally he completely lost his temper with me and went up on deck. I stayed in the cabin for a little while and then decided to join him. (*A moment*) To my surprise, I couldn't find him. He wasn't on deck or in any of the public rooms. I searched the entire boat; I searched everywhere; but I just couldn't find him. In the end, of course, I had to send for the Captain. (*Another pause*) The next day, as you can well imagine, I was utterly and completely bewildered. I just didn't know what on earth to do. Finally, I flew back to Marseilles.

PETER: It must have been terrible for you.

PHYLLIS: Yes, it was. And the newspapers didn't exactly help, I'm afraid.

Pause.

PETER: (*At a loss; almost as if searching for something to say*) Did you ever find the doll?

PHYLLIS: After the accident I forgot all about it; it went completely out of my mind. Then one night … (*Pause*) I was staying at a small hotel just off La Canabiere and one night, after I'd been for a walk, I went into the bathroom and … there it was.

22

PETER: The doll?

PHYLLIS: Yes. While I'd been out someone had filled the bath and the doll was floating on top of the water.

PETER: (*Incredulously*) The same doll?

PHYLLIS: Yes, I think it was the same doll, it certainly looked like it. About an hour later, the police telephoned me. I was asked to identify my husband's body. It had been washed up on the beach.

PETER: (*Staggered*) Why – that's an incredible story! Did you tell the police what had happened? I mean – about the doll?

PHYLLIS: Yes, I did. They simply took possession of it and said nothing. Whether the doll was important or not, I don't know. They didn't tell me, and I didn't ask them. I just wanted to leave Marseilles. To get back to America. To get home.

PETER: My God, yes – I can well understand that.

PHYLLIS: Well, that's it, Mr Matty. Now you know the whole story. (*There is a pause, then PHYLLIS rises and somewhat to PETER's surprise shakes hands with him*) Thank you for the drink.

PHYLLIS leaves the table and a puzzled PETER stares after her. The waiter appears and presents the check. As PETER slowly sits down again and takes out his wallet, we hear his voice.

PETER: (*Voice over*) The moment she left I knew, that, no matter what happened, I simply had to see her again. So, the very next morning, as soon as I arrived at the office, I telephoned her.

CUT TO: PETER MATTY's Office. Day.

PETER is standing by his desk, on the phone. As the conversation with PHYLLIS proceeds, he looks faintly surprised and then obviously delighted.

PETER: (*Voice over*) I told her that I was going to do some work on my boat over the weekend and since Poole was only about twelve miles from Heatherdown – why didn't she let me drive her down there? I expected her to refuse my offer, but much to my surprise she didn't. On the contrary, she appeared grateful for the suggestion. I picked her up at the hotel early on Friday afternoon.

CUT TO: Connaught Hotel, London. Day.

PETER's Jaguar draws up to the hotel and he gets out of the driving seat. As he does so LINDA BRAITHWAITE comes out of the hotel and crosses to a waiting taxi.

LINDA: (*Suddenly noticing PETER*) Hello, Mr Matty! Phyllis is ready, she'll be with you in a minute.

PETER: Oh – thank you.

LINDA: I've just been saying goodbye to her. I'm flying back to the States this evening – and very sorry to be leaving, I might add.

PETER: You'll have to pay us another visit.

LINDA: I certainly will. I'm crazy about London. But who isn't? Nice to have seen you again. Have a lovely weekend and take care of Phyllis.

LINDA gets into the taxi. PHYLLIS appears at this moment, followed by a porter carrying her suitcase. She waves to LINDA as her taxi pulls away from the hotel, then she joins PETER.

PHYLLIS: Sorry if I'm late.

PETER: I've just arrived.

PHYLLIS: Is it going to keep fine?

PETER: I think so.

PETER nods to the porter and points to the boot of the car.

PHYLLIS: (*Watching the porter as he puts her case in the boot*) My goodness, what a lovely car!

PETER: (*Offering her the car key*) It's all yours!

PHYLLIS: What do you mean?

PETER: You said you were crazy about driving.

PHYLLIS: I am.

PETER: Well – I hate it. So go ahead. You drive.

PHYLLIS: Why do people who hate driving always have the nicest cars? (*Looking at the key; obviously pleased by PETER's suggestion*) Are you serious?

PETER: Absolutely!

PHYLLIS: What happens if I smash into something?

PETER: I shall bale out!

As PHYLLIS laughs, PETER tips the porter and opens the car door for her.

CUT TO: Country Road. Day.

The Jaguar, being driven by Phyllis, along a country road.

CUT TO: Inside PETER's car. Day.

PHYLLIS is at the wheel of the car, obviously enjoying herself.

PHYLLIS: It really is a fabulous car. It handles beautifully.

PETER: You're a very good driver.

PHYLLIS: For a woman …

PETER: You said it! What are your other accomplishments? Are you any good on boats?

PHYLLIS: (*Laughing*) No! I hardly know the difference between the bow and the stern.

PETER: I'm delighted to hear it. That means I can
                    really shoot a line.

CUT TO: Country Road. Day. Later in the afternoon.
*PETER's car is being driven by PHYLLIS. From time to time,
PETER steals a glance at her.*

CUT TO: Inside PETER's Car. Day.
PHYLLIS: It can't be far now, according to that last
                    signpost.
PETER: No; about thirty miles, that's all. Tired?
PHYLLIS: Not a bit. I'm enjoying every minute of it.
                    (*PHYLLIS looks at PETER*)
PETER: So am I.

CUT TO: The entrance to Poole Harbour. Day.
*PHYLLIS at the wheel of the Jaguar as it approaches the
Marina. PETER is pointing out one of the landmarks.*

CUT TO: Poole Harbour. Day.
*PETER's boat, "First Edition", is moored. PETER steps back
from the quayside onto the deck of his boat. PHYLLIS stands
on the quay looking at the boat. PETER's car is in the
background.*
PETER: Do you like it?
PHYLLIS: Yes, I do … (*PHYLLIS looks at the name*)
                    First Edition.
PETER: (*Laughing*) Frightfully original. One of
                    our authors suggested it should be called
                    "Out of Print".
PETER holds out a hand to help PHYLLIS aboard.
PHYLLIS: I don't know much about boats, I'm afraid.
PETER: Right – then we'll have the first lesson.
                    (*Pointing*) That's the stern, and that's the

bow. (*Faking*) Is it? No, wait a minute! I've got that wrong! That's the stern, and that's the bow.

PHYLLIS laughs. They are standing quite close now, looking at each other.

PETER: (*Breaking the spell*) What time did you say you'd get to Heatherdown?

PHYLLIS: I said about … half-past three or four.

PETER: (*Looking at his watch*) That's fine. I'll show you the rest of the boat and then we'll drive over there.

PHYLLIS: Peter, there's no need for you to come. I can easily pick up a cab …

PETER: Nonsense! If you think I'm going to let you … (*A sudden thought*) Wait a minute! I'll tell you what you can do! You can borrow the car.

PHYLLIS: No, really – I couldn't do that.

PETER: Why not? It's a splendid idea! That way I'm bound to see you again because you'll have to bring it back. No, seriously – it's a very good suggestion. Supposing you don't like this Sir Arnold character?

PHYLLIS: I'm sure I will.

PETER: Yes, I'm sure too, but – just supposing you don't? Then all you've got to do is tell him about your friends in Bournemouth, jump in the car, and come straight back here.

PHYLLIS: What friends in Bournemouth?

PETER: Such old, old friends. They'd be very upset if you decided to stay anywhere else.

A moment.

PHYLLIS: (*The flicker of a smile*) You sound very experienced at this sort of thing, Mr Matty.

27

PETER: Oh, but I am. I've got girl friends all over
                    the place. When you've been down below,
                    I'll take you round the corner and
                    introduce you to one of them.

*PETER takes hold of PHYLLIS's arm and leads her towards
the galley.*

CUT TO: Village Post Office. Day.

This is a sweet-shop-cum-stationers-cum-newsagents-cum-
post office. There is a telephone box near the counter.

*MRS FRINTON, a stout, jolly woman in her early sixties, is
just putting some articles into a bag for a customer.*

MRS FRINTON: There we are. Oh, and the labels, wasn't
                    it? That'll be nineteen pence altogether,
                    please.

*The customer pays, picks up the bag and moves to the door,
passing PETER and PHYLLIS who have just entered the shop.*

PETER: Hello, Mrs Frinton. How are you today?

MRS FRINTON: Oh, Mr Matty – you down here again
                    then?

PETER: That's right. I've got one or two jobs to do
                    on the boat.

MRS FRINTON: You've got some nice weather for it.

PETER: Makes a change, doesn't it? Oh – Mrs
                    Frinton – this is a friend of mine. Mrs Du
                    Salle.

MRS FRINTON: Pleased to meet you.

PHYLLIS smiles at MRS FRINTON.

PETER: Mrs   Du   Salle's   going   over   to
                    Heatherdown to visit some friends of hers,
                    and I've arranged for her to telephone you
                    this evening and leave a message for me.
                    Is that convenient?

MRS FRINTON: Yes, of course, dearie. No problem.

MRS FRINTON picks up a pencil and writes down her telephone number on a sweet bag and offers it to PHYLLIS.

PHYLLIS: (*Taking the bag*) Thank you. (*Looking at the number*) Poole 89567.

MRS FRINTON: That's right, my dear. Don't worry. I'll see he gets the message.

PHYLLIS: It'll probably be about six o'clock when I phone.

MRS FRINTON: I'll be here. (*To PETER*) I'll pop up to the boat.

CUT TO: Outside the Post Office. Day.

PHYLLIS, in PETER's car, starts the engine, waves and drives off. As the car pulls away, we see PETER standing on the kerb, waving after her.

PETER: (*Voice over*) She took my car and left for Heatherdown as arranged. Feeling distinctly pleased with the way things had turned out, I went back to the boat and did one or two odd jobs.

CUT TO: Poole Harbour. Day.

PETER is on his boat, painting one of the lifebelts. He pauses in his work, smiling to himself. He waves a friendly greeting to a passer-by on the quay.

PETER: (*Voice over*) At about ten minutes past six I decided not to wait for Mrs Frinton but to stroll down to the post office.

PETER looks at his watch, makes a decision, stabs the paint brush into the pot, and jumps onto the quayside, walking briskly away.

CUT TP: The Post Office. Day.

PETER is standing at the closed door of the Post Office,
waiting.

PETER: (*Voice over*) The post office was closed, of
                    course, but as you know, Mrs Frinton lives
                    on the premises. She said Phyllis hadn't
                    telephoned …

We see MRS FRINTON opening the Post Office door and
talking to PETER. PETER nods rather wistfully and gives a
little nod as he walks away.

PETER: (*Voice over*) … But she assured me that
                    the moment there was a message she
                    would deliver it to the boat.

CUT TO: Poole Harbour. Evening.

PETER is sitting disconsolately on the deck of his boat.

PETER: (*Voice over*) I sat on deck that evening just
                    waiting for Mrs Frinton to turn up. But she
                    didn't. She didn't for the very good reason
                    that Phyllis hadn't contacted her. Finally, I
                    came to the conclusion that Sir Arnold had
                    prevailed upon Phyllis to stay the night
                    and that somehow, she just hadn't been
                    able to telephone. I made up my mind that
                    if I didn't receive a message from her by
                    eleven o'clock the next morning, I'd
                    telephone her myself.

CUT TO: Outside the Post Office. Morning.

PETER is crossing the road and going into the shop.

CUT TO: Inside the Post Office. Morning.

MRS FRINTON, her glasses on, is doing her Post Office
accounts. She looks up as PETER enters.

MRS FRINTON: Good morning, Mr Matty. No message
                yet, I'm afraid, from that friend of yours.
PETER: I see. Thank you, Mrs Frinton. May I see
                your local directory?

*MRS FRINTON picks up a telephone book from amongst a
pile of newspapers, magazines, etc.*

MRS FRINTON: Yes, of course. Here we are. Heatherdown
                you wanted, wasn't it?
PETER: Yes. Thank you.

*As PETER opens the directory there is the sound of an
approaching car. He is searching for the number when the
car passes the shop. PETER looks up.*

CUT TO: Outside the Post Office. Morning.

*PETER's Jaguar races past the shop. PETER comes running
out of the shop and stares after the car. After a momentary
hesitation, he smiles and runs lightly in the direction of the
quay.*

CUT TO: Poole Harbour. Morning.

The quayside where PETER's car is parked.

*PETER walks quickly towards his car, stops a few yards
away, slightly breathless from hurrying. He looks faintly
puzzled. We see that there is no one inside the car. PETER
moves to the edge of the quay staring down at the boat. There
is no one on the boat either. PETER looks around him,
puzzled, wondering where PHYLLIS has got to.*

POLICEMAN: (*Out of view*) Good morning.

*PETER turns with a start, looking down at the POLICEMAN
who is emerging from the cabin of his boat.*

PETER: Good morning.
POLICEMAN: This your boat, sir?
PETER: Yes, it is.

31

POLICEMAN: Then you're Mr Matty, and I take it that's
               your car over there?

PETER: Yes … Look – what's happened? What's
               this all about?

*The POLICEMAN steps onto the quay now as a police car
approaches. PETER turns and stares at the police car as it
comes to a halt.*

POLICEMAN: Was your car stolen, sir?

PETER: No, of course it wasn't! If it had been
               stolen, I'd have reported it. I lent it to a
               friend of mine.

*The POLICEMAN is fishing in his pocket. PETER is
becoming impatient now.*

PETER: Look – would you please tell me what
               you're doing with my car?

*The POLICEMAN hands PETER the piece of paper he has
taken from his pocket. PETER looks at it.*

PETER: (*Reading*) Please return this car to Mr
               Peter Matty, c/o Yacht "First Edition",
               Poole Harbour …

PETER looks at the POLICEMAN, puzzled.

POLICEMAN: That was on the windscreen. The car was
               found in a private lane leading to a farm at
               Landon Cross.

PETER: Landon Cross?

POLICEMAN: About a mile and a half from
               Heatherdown.

PETER nods, taken aback by the news.

POLICEMAN: You say you lent your car to a friend?

PETER: That's right. She was visiting someone in
               Heatherdown.

The POLICEMAN gives PETER a meaning look.

POLICEMAN: Yes, well – it's a very nice car, sir. I'd be
               careful who I lent it to in future.

	Incidentally, your friend went off with the key. We had a devil of a job finding another one. Have you got a spare?
PETER:	(*Nodding; obviously bewildered*) Yes, I have.
POLICEMAN:	(*Handing PETER a key*) Well – you might as well have this one. It's no longer any use to us.
PETER:	(*Taking the key; his thoughts elsewhere*) Thank you. And thank you for returning the car, Officer.
POLICEMAN:	It was a pleasure driving it. Wish it was mine.

The POLICEMAN gives a friendly nod and joins his colleague in the waiting police car. PETER stares after the police car as it drives off. Then, distinctly puzzled, he looks at the note in his hand – the note that was left on the windscreen of his car.

PETER:	(*Voice over*) I just didn't know what to make of this new development. Obviously, Phyllis must have had second thoughts about returning to the boat. But even so – why didn't she simply telephone Mrs Frinton and arrange for me to pick up the car? Frankly, Claude, I was bewildered. I just couldn't understand it! I began to wonder if I'd unwittingly offended her in some way or other. Finally, I decided that the only thing to do was to visit Forest Gate Manor in the hope that Sir Arnold, or perhaps Phyllis herself, might be able to throw some light on the mystery. So, after burning some bacon and

eggs in the galley, I drove over to
Heatherdown.

CUT TO: High Street. Heatherdown. Day.
*PETER's car is moving slowly through the High Street. It
stops and PETER leans out to address a woman wheeling a
shopping trolley. In the near background we see several
shops, including that of MORTIMER BROWN, Photographer.
The woman points, giving PETER instructions on how to find
Forest Gate Manor. PETER thanks her and the car drives off.*

CUT TO: Forest Gate Manor, Heatherdown. Day.
*PETER's car turns in at the drive which is attractively
hedged, and stops outside the lovely old house. PETER gets
out of the car, looks around at the pleasant, quiet
surroundings. He goes to the front door and rings the bell.
He waits, glancing up at the trees, listening to the birds.
PETER rings the bell again. He waits. He is about to ring it
for the third time when the door is opened by MRS CASSIDY,
SIR ARNOLD's housekeeper. She is about fifty, sharp-
featured, tall, efficient, and somewhat precise in manner. As
the door opens, we hear the sound of a piano being played.*
MRS CASSIDY: Yes? What is it?
PETER: Could I speak to Sir Arnold Wyatt, please?
MRS CASSIDY: Have you an appointment?
PETER: No, I'm afraid I haven't. My name is
Matty. Peter Matty.
*MRS CASSIDY looks at PETER, obviously studying his
clothes, his general air of affluence. When she has finished
weighing him up, she looks at the car.*
MRS CASSIDY: Just a moment, please.
*MRS CASSIDY disappears into the house. PETER stands at
the door, waiting. He suddenly becomes aware of the fact that
he is being watched, and turning he sees a little girl standing*

on the drive, some distance away, quietly staring at him. She is an appealing child of about five years old. MRS CASSIDY reappears at the door.

MRS CASSIDY: Sir Arnold will see you. Please come this way.

PETER steps inside, glancing back at the child as he does so. MRS CASSIDY closes the door.

CUT TO: SIR ARNOLD WYATT's Study at Forest Gate Manor. Day.

SIR ARNOLD WYATT is listening to music on the record player. A Beethoven Concerto, played by CLAUDE MATTY. As PETER is shown into the room by MRS CASSIDY, he stops the music and turns towards his visitor.

SIR ARNOLD WYATT is in his early sixties. A shrewd, studious looking man with a faintly disarming manner. As MRS CASSIDY goes out PETER notices several LPs on the table near the fireplace; he recognises his brother's photograph on several of the sleeves.

WYATT: Mr Matty?

PETER: Yes.

WYATT: I'm Sir Arnold Wyatt. What can I do for you, sir?

PETER: I'm a friend of Mrs Du Salle's. I expect she mentioned my name to you yesterday afternoon. I lent Phyllis – Mrs Du Salle – my car and I was wondering why she abandoned it.

WYATT: (*Stopping PETER*) Mrs Du Salle?

PETER: Yes.

WYATT: (*Puzzled*) I'm sorry, Mr Matty, but I think there's some mistake. I don't know anyone of that name.

PETER stares at WYATT.

PETER: But she came here yesterday afternoon! You invited her for the weekend!

WYATT: I did?

PETER: Yes.

WYATT: But … I've never heard of Mrs Du Salle. (*Puzzled; indicating a chair*) Sit down, sir. Please …

PETER hesitates, then crosses to the settee.

WYATT: Now, would you be kind enough to explain what this is all about?

PETER: I've told you. It's about Phyllis Du Salle.

WYATT: (*A shade irritated*) Yes, I know. You said that!

PETER: She married a friend of yours – a very close friend.

WYATT: A friend of mine?

PETER: Yes. Norman Du Salle.

WYATT looks puzzled and shakes his head.

WYATT: I'm sorry, sir …

PETER: (*Exasperated*) Look – you must have heard of Norman Du Salle! He was a journalist. He emigrated to America …

WYATT: (*Faintly resenting PETER's tone; with a note of authority*) I'm sorry, but I haven't heard of any of these people! And if you'll forgive my saying so, I haven't heard of you either! Now what's this all about and who are you, exactly?

PETER looks at SIR ARNOLD for a moment; he is beginning to be impressed by WYATT's bewilderment.

PETER: My name is Peter Matty. I'm a book publisher. And if you haven't heard of me, you've certainly heard of my brother.

PETER points to the collection of LPs.

WYATT: (*Surprised*) Claude Matty? He's your brother?

PETER: Yes. (*Takes out his wallet and hands Wyatt his card*)

36

WYATT: I'm a great admirer of your brother, Mr Matty. He's given me a lot of pleasure over the years. He has indeed. (*He looks at the card*) Matty Publications! Why, yes, of course! (*More friendly*) Forgive me if I seemed a little abrupt just now, but – well, to be frank, I'm utterly bewildered by what you've just told me. Who is this – Mrs Du Salle? And what gave you the idea that she was a friend of mine?

PETER: I met her on a plane coming back from Geneva. We got talking. She told me that it was her first visit to England and that she was very much looking forward to meeting you. She said you were a very close friend, a very dear friend, of her late husband's.

WYATT: But this is nonsense! I assure you I've never even heard of the young lady! But please – go on, Mr Matty.

PETER: I have a boat in Poole Harbour and since I was coming down here for the weekend, I suggested she came down with me. And – well, that's about it. Except that I lent her my car to drive over here.

WYATT: When was this?

PETER: Yesterday afternoon. The car was returned to me early this morning.

WYATT: (*Puzzled*) By Mrs Du Salle?

PETER: No, by the police. Apparently, she left it in a deserted lane not far from here.

WYATT: Well – this really is quite extraordinary! I just don't understand it! You say, you met the young lady coming back from Geneva?

PETER: Yes. I'd been to a concert given by my brother.

WYATT: And you … got friendly with her?

PETER: Yes, I suppose you could put it that way.

37

WYATT: Did she – forgive my asking – but did she borrow money from you?

PETER: Good heavens, no! She wouldn't even let me take her out to dinner.

WYATT: Well, this is quite beyond me! I must confess, I really don't know what on earth to say to you! I just can't imagine what this young lady was up to!

PETER hesitates, looks at WYATT for a moment, then making a decision, rises and holds out his hand.

PETER: My apologies for troubling you. I've taken up quite enough of your time.

WYATT: (*Shaking hands with PETER*) If your brother ever finds himself in this part of the world, Mr Matty, I'd be more than delighted to make his acquaintance.

CUT TO: Outside of Forest Gate Manor. Day.

PETER comes out of the house and crosses to his car. As he gets into the car, he nods goodbye to WYATT who is now standing in the doorway. WYATT acknowledges the nod and goes back into the house, closing the door behind him.

PETER: (*Voice over*) I said goodbye to Sir Arnold and returned to the boat. As I drove down the drive towards the main road, I suddenly saw the little girl again. She was standing on the lawn …

PETER's car goes down the drive. As it approaches the entrance, he notices the child again, standing on the lawn watching him. She has an attractive doll in her arms; the doll is wearing a Tyrolean costume. PETER's eyes are on the little girl as the car continues slowly down the drive.

CUT TO: PETER MATTY's Office. Day.

PETER is now standing with his back to CLAUDE, staring out of the window. He is finishing his story.

PETER: I stayed on the boat for about ten days in the hope that she would contact me, or at least get in touch with Mrs Frinton. But she didn't. In the end – desperately unhappy – I came back to London. (*PETER turns from the window and looks at CLAUDE*) All this happened just over three weeks ago. And I've been desperately unhappy ever since.

A slight pause.

CLAUDE: My God, you really have fallen for her, haven't you! There's nothing like a confirmed bachelor for …

PETER: Making a damn fool of himself!

CLAUDE: (*Quietly*) No, I wasn't going to say that.

PETER: If only she'd write to me, or phone … or at least offer some sort of an explanation.

CLAUDE: (*Thoughtfully*) I suppose she did stay at the Connaught?

PETER: Yes, I checked with the hotel. I wondered if she'd left a forwarding address, but she hadn't.

CLAUDE: What about Max Lerner?

PETER: Max?

CLAUDE: Yes. Have you spoken to him about this? Didn't she tell you that they'd once met?

PETER: Yes, she did. But he certainly doesn't remember meeting her.

CLAUDE: Well, the only thing I can suggest, dear boy, is – try and forget the whole episode. But that doesn't help very much, I'm afraid.

PETER shakes his head and crosses down to the desk.

PETER: When do you propose going down to the boat?

CLAUDE: This evening …
PETER: (*Surprised*) This evening?
CLAUDE: Yes, if that's all right with you?
PETER: Yes, of course.
CLAUDE: I know what'll happen if I stay in Town. The phone will start ringing and I'll get involved, which means I won't have a minute to myself.
PETER: Yes, I'm sure you're right. I'll join you on Saturday morning. Friday night if possible.
CLAUDE: (*Putting his arm on PETER's shoulder*) It'll be like old times. I gather from what you've told me, Mrs Frinton is still around?
PETER: (*His thoughts elsewhere*) Yes – she's still around.

CUT TO: A London Street. Night.
A taxi draws up at the kerb. PETER gets out. He speaks to someone inside the taxi.
PETER: I'm going down to the boat at the weekend. I'll give you a ring when I get back.
We now see that the other occupant of the taxi is MAX LERNER.
MAX: Yes, all right, old boy. Thanks for the dinner. And the cheque. My ex-wife – wives, I should say – will be delighted.
PETER: Good night, Max.
The taxi pulls away. PETER goes up the steps to the front door of the house. As he puts the key in the lock, we see the list of names and bell pushes at the side of the porch indicating that the house is arranged into flats.

CUT TO: The Living Room of PETER's Flat. Night.
PETER's bachelor flat is tastefully furnished if faintly untidy.

PETER enters, yawns, takes off his jacket and loosens his tie. He switches on the radio.

CUT TO: The Bedroom. Night.
PETER enters, takes off his shirt, and puts on his dressing gown. There is a pile of new books on his bedside table. He picks up the top one, looks approvingly at the design of the jacket, yawns again, and tosses it back onto the table. He goes into the adjoining bathroom.

CUT TO: The Bathroom. Night.
PETER enters, takes his toothbrush from the holder. He looks idly at his reflection in the mirror as he turns on the water tap. He suddenly reacts to seeing something else in the reflection in the mirror. He turns sharply to stare at the bath. The camera pans to the bath and we see that it is filled with water. A child's doll is floating on the top of the water, moving ever so slowly along the surface. PETER stares at the doll in amazement. It looks remarkably like the doll belonging to the little girl at Forest Gate Manor. PETER continues to stare at the doll, transfixed. He suddenly realises that the doorbell is ringing.

CUT TO: The Hall of PETER's Flat. Night.
PETER comes out of the living room, passes through the hall, and opens the front door. A tall, serious looking man is standing in the doorway.

SEATON: Mr Matty?
PETER: Yes?
SEATON: Could you spare me a few moments, sir? My name is Seaton. Detective-Inspector Seaton. (*He shows PETER his C.I.D. identity card*)
PETER: Yes, of course. Come along in, Inspector.

CUT TO: The Living Room of PETER's Flat. Night.

The INSPECTOR enters followed by PETER.

SEATON: I understand you have a Jaguar, sir?

PETER: (*Puzzled*) Yes, I have.

SEATON: Registration number NPE 277L?

PETER: Yes, that's right.

SEATON: Then I rather imagine this is yours, sir. (*He produces a car key attached to a plastic disc*) It's got your car number on it.

PETER takes the key and looks at it.

PETER: Yes, this is mine. Where did you find it?

SEATON: Did you lose it, sir?

PETER: No, I gave it to someone. (*Tensely*) Where did you find it?

A slight pause.

SEATON: A woman was picked out of the Thames, near Deptford, early this afternoon. That key was in her possession.

PETER is obviously shaken.

PETER: Picked out of … You mean, she's dead?

SEATON: Yes, sir. She'd been shot and her body dumped in the river.

PETER: (*A moment; quietly*) I think you'll find her name is Du Salle. About three weeks ago she borrowed my car and … forgot to return the key.

SEATON: (*Shaking his head*) No, sir. We've established who she is. We just wondered if, by any chance, you could add anything further to our information.

PETER looks at SEATON.

SEATON: Her name is Braithwaite. Linda Braithwaite. She's an American.

CUT TO: Forest Gate Manor, Heatherdown. Day.

PETER's car enters the drive and finally stops outside the house. PETER gets out of the Jaguar and crosses to the front door. He carries a small zip carrier. As PETER approaches the front door it suddenly opens, and MRS CASSIDY appears.

MRS CASSIDY: Oh – Mr Matty.

PETER: Good afternoon. Is Sir Arnold at home?

MRS CASSIDY: Er – yes, I think so. Please come in.

PETER goes into the house and MRS CASSIDY closes the front door behind them.

CUT TO: The Hall of Forest Gate Manor. Day.

PETER stands just inside the hall. MRS CASSIDY is moving towards the study when SIR ARNOLD comes through the door to the study.

WYATT: Yes, Mrs Cassidy? Who – (*He sees PETER standing there*) Why, Mr Matty!

PETER: Good afternoon. I hope I'm not disturbing you …

WYATT: Not at all. Do come in … Thank you, Mrs Cassidy.

WYATT waves his hand and PETER goes into the study. WYATT follows him in. MRS CASSIDY stands there looking after them.

CUT TO: The Study. Day.

PETER enters with WYATT.

WYATT: Please sit down, Mr Matty.

PETER: Thank you.

WYATT: Well, did you find the young lady you were looking for?

PETER: No, I'm afraid I didn't.

WYATT: I was talking to Mrs Cassidy – my housekeeper – about it after you left, and

	we really couldn't think who she could possibly have been. It really was an extraordinary story.
PETER:	Sir Arnold, when I was last here, I noticed a little girl playing on the lawn.
WYATT:	Yes. That was Sarah. My granddaughter.
PETER:	She had a doll in her arms. A rather pretty little doll.
WYATT:	(*Puzzled*) Yes, that's very likely. I know the doll you mean.
PETER:	Has she, by any chance, lost it?
WYATT:	Lost it? You mean, the doll?
PETER:	Yes.
WYATT:	I don't think so.
PETER:	Because if she has, I think I've found it.

PETER opens the zip carrier and produces the doll he found in his bathroom.

WYATT:	(*Surprised; staring at the doll*) Yes, that's Sarah's! Where did you find it, on the drive?
PETER:	No, I found it last night. Someone left it in my flat.
WYATT:	(*Astonished*) In your flat? But why on earth should anyone do that?
PETER:	I don't know. I can't imagine why. I simply went into the bathroom before going to bed and there it was.
WYATT:	Wait a minute! Last night, you say?

PETER nods.

WYATT:	But I'm sure I saw Sarah playing with her doll this morning.
PETER:	(*Looking at the doll*) Then maybe we're both mistaken and this isn't the same doll.

WYATT: It looks remarkably like it. Yes, I'm sure it's
            Sarah's! I'll have a word with my housekeeper.
            (*He crosses and picks up the internal phone;
            presses a button*) … Mrs Cassidy, would you
            send Sarah along to the study, please. Yes,
            straight away. (*He replaces the phone*)

PETER: Does your little granddaughter live at
            Heatherdown?

WYATT looks at PETER, faintly surprised by the question.

WYATT: She lives here, Mr Matty, with me. Her parents
            are dead.

PETER: Oh! I didn't realise that.

WYATT: No, of course not. Why should you? My
            daughter and her husband were killed in a plane
            crash.

PETER: I'm sorry, I …

WYATT: As a matter of fact, this doll, if it's the one we
            think it is, arrived for Sarah the very day the
            accident happened. It was Sarah's birthday and
            her father, my son-in-law, sent it to her from
            Vienna.

PETER: (*Not quite sure what to say*) It must be a great
            responsibility looking after a little girl.

WYATT: It is, and I'm not getting any younger, I'm afraid.
            But she's a delightful child and fortunately Mrs
            Cassidy is devoted to her. (*A moment*) You
            probably read about the accident. The plane
            crashed near Innsbruck, just after take-off.
            (*Pause*) I was very devoted to my daughter. She
            was an only child.

*There is a rap on the study door and WYATT crosses the
room and opens it. The little girl – Sarah – is standing in the
doorway holding her doll. It is a replica of the one PETER is*

holding. WYATT smiles at SARAH, then taking the doll out of her arms he crosses down to PETER.

WYATT: We appear to have been mistaken, Mr Matty.

CUT TO: The Cabin of First Edition. Poole Harbour. Night.
PETER and CLAUDE have just finished their evening meal. PETER looks worried and is obviously slightly on edge. The doll is on the table near the coffee percolator.

PETER: Sorry about the meal, it hasn't been very good, I'm afraid.

CLAUDE: Not to worry.

PETER: We'll drive into Heatherdown tomorrow morning and do some shopping.

A slight pause.

CLAUDE: You know, I still don't understand why you didn't tell the Inspector about the doll.

PETER: I didn't tell him about it because I thought I knew who it belonged to. Also, it was such a complicated story I just didn't think he'd believe me.

CLAUDE: But someone broke into your flat, Peter!

PETER: (*Shaking his head*) No-one broke into the flat. Whoever planted the doll obviously had a key and simply let himself into the apartment.

CLAUDE: How many keys are there?

PETER: Two. I've got one and Mrs Galloway, my daily, has the other one.

CLAUDE: Has she still got it?

PETER: Yes, she has. I checked.

CLAUDE: You haven't given anyone else a key? (*Looking at PETER*) Recently, I mean?

PETER: No, I've just told you, there's only … (*Suddenly realising what CLAUDE is getting at*) Look,

Claude – I told you the truth about Phyllis Du
Salle.

CLAUDE: (*Still looking at PETER*) The whole truth?

PETER: Yes, the whole truth! I didn't sleep with her and I
didn't give her a key to my apartment, if that's
what you're thinking!

CLAUDE: All right, old boy! All right. Fair enough. (*A
moment*) But the thing I find very puzzling is the
fact that you found the doll – <u>a</u> doll – under
almost exactly the same circumstances as Mrs
Du Salle.

PETER: Yes, I know.

CLAUDE: Have you examined the doll?

PETER: Examined it? What do you mean?

CLAUDE: Well – have you looked inside it?

PETER stares at CLAUDE.

PETER: No, of course I haven't!

CLAUDE: Don't you think it might be a good idea if you
did?

PETER quietly picks up the doll and looks at it.

PETER: You think … there might be something hidden
inside it?

CLAUDE: It's possible. If there is – it could explain a great
deal.

PETER: Well, we'll soon find out!

*PETER hands CLAUDE the doll and, rising, crosses to a
nearby cupboard. As CLAUDE examines the doll, PETER
searches in the cupboard, finally discovering what he is
looking for – a large Swiss pocket-knife. He returns to the
table and, taking the doll from CLAUDE, begins to
disembowel it. Gradually the doll is torn apart, the inside
wadding being strewn across the table. PETER and CLAUDE
carefully, methodically, examine every piece of the doll.
Pause.*

47

CLAUDE: There's nothing here, I'm afraid.

PETER: No. (*Pause*) Wait a minute, what's this? (*Examining a piece of the wadding*) No, it's nothing …

CLAUDE suddenly puts his hand on PETER's arm. He has obviously heard something.

CLAUDE: Listen! There's someone coming …

Pause.

MRS FRINTON: (*Calling from outside*) Anybody at home?

PETER: It's Mrs Frinton! (*Calling*) Come along down, Mrs Frinton!

After a moment, MRS FRINTON appears. She is dressed for all seasons.

MRS FRINTON: Sorry to disturb you, Mr Matty.

PETER: That's all right. What can we do for you? Oh – I think you know my brother.

MRS FRINTON is staring at the disembowelled doll.

MRS FRINTON: Yes, o' course. (*To CLAUDE*) Good evening, Mr Matty. I heard you were down here. Nice to see you again.

CLAUDE: Thank you, Mrs Frinton. You look very well.

MRS FRINTON: Well, I'm not too bad, sir, all things considering. (*Finally taking her eyes off the table; to PETER*) There's been a message for you. That friend of yours telephoned at last.

PETER: Friend of mine? (*Suddenly; rising*) You don't mean – Mrs Du Salle?

MRS FRINTON: She didn't leave her name, but I'm sure it's the call you've been expecting. She wants you to ring her back. I've got the number somewhere … (*Feeling in her pockets*) Oh dear – what on earth did I do

48

	with it? Ah, here we are! (*Produces a piece of paper which PETER immediately snatches from her*)
PETER:	(*Reading from the piece of paper*) Heatherdown 98064?
MRS FRINTON:	That's right, dearie.
PETER:	(*Quickly*) What else did she say, Mrs Frinton?
MRS FRINTON:	She asked me if you were staying down here. I said I wasn't certain, but I felt sure you'd be coming because your brother was already here.
PETER:	Claude, I'll be back in ten minutes! Come along, Mrs Frinton, I want to use your phone!

CUT TO: Inside the Post Office. Evening.
MRS FRINTON lets herself into the post office, followed by PETER. He immediately enters the phone box as MRS FRINTON crosses behind the counter.

CUT TO: Inside the Telephone Box in the Post Office. Evening.
PETER picks up the phone and carefully dials a number. The number rings out for some little time before we finally hear MRS CASSIDY's voice on the other end. We do not see her; we stay with PETER during this entire telephone conversation. PETER inserts some coins.

MRS CASSIDY:	Hello? … Who is that? …
PETER:	Hello … Heatherdown 98064?
MRS CASSIDY:	Yes, speaking …
PETER:	Could I speak to Mrs Du Salle, please?

A slight pause.

MRS CASSIDY:	I beg your pardon?

PETER:	Are you Heatherdown 98064?
MRS CASSIDY:	Yes.
PETER:	Well – could I speak to Mrs Du Salle please?
MRS CASSIDY:	(*After a moment*) I think you've got the wrong number.
PETER:	Heatherdown 98064?
MRS CASSIDY:	That's right. Who is it speaking?
PETER:	(*Impatiently*) My name is Matty. I'm a friend of Mrs Du Salle's and I wish to speak to her. (*A definite pause*) Hello?
MRS CASSIDY:	Will you hold on, please?

PETER looks at the receiver in his hand, puzzled. He now realises that MRS CASSIDY's voice is vaguely familiar. A pause – then WYATT's voice is heard.

WYATT:	This is Sir Arnold Wyatt speaking. Can I help you?
PETER:	(*Taken aback*) Sir Arnold?
WYATT:	Yes – has something happened, Mr Matty? My housekeeper seems a little confused.
PETER:	I – I received a message asking me to ring your number.
WYATT:	There must be some mistake. I left no message for you. Are you sure you got the right number?
PETER:	Yes, I think so.
WYATT:	Who is it you wanted to speak to?
PETER:	(*Hesitating*) Mrs Du Salle …
WYATT:	Mrs Du Salle!
PETER:	Yes. She telephoned a friend of mine and … left a message for me to ring her back.
WYATT:	(*Astonished*) At this number? Heatherdown 98064?
PETER:	Well – yes.

WYATT: Mr Matty, either your friend got hold of
                       the wrong number or someone is quite
                       deliberately trying to make a fool out of
                       you. Frankly, in view of what's happened,
                       I'm inclined to think the latter.

*PETER hesitates, is about to say something, then looks at the
receiver and slowly replaces it.*

CUT TO: Inside the Post Office. Evening.

*PETER comes out of the phone box and thoughtfully crosses
to the counter and MRS FRINTON.*

PETER: (*Showing MRS FRINTON the piece of
                       paper*) Mrs Frinton, are you sure you
                       didn't make a mistake with this number?

MRS FRINTON: I'm quite sure. I wrote it down straight
                       away. Didn't you get hold of your friend?

PETER: (*Thoughtfully*) No, she wasn't there.
                       (*Looking at MRS FRINTON*) You're
                       absolutely sure about the number?

MRS FRINTON: Positive. She repeated it twice, dearie. I
                       promise you, I wrote it down straight
                       away.

*PETER gives a puzzled nod and, still staring at the piece of
paper, walks slowly towards the door.*

CUT TO: Main Steet of Heatherdown. Morning.

*CLAUDE is standing outside a café – FLETCHER's CAFÉ –
waiting for PETER. He suddenly sees PETER on the other
side of the street. PETER can be seen walking towards his
parked car; he is carrying two large bags of shopping. He
stops at the car and puts the shopping into the boot. Having
closed the boot, he crosses the road and joins CLAUDE.*

PETER: Sorry, it took longer than I thought.
CLAUDE: Do you feel like a coffee?

PETER: Yes – why not? I'll join you inside, I'm just
           going to get some cigarettes.

*CLAUDE nods and goes into the café. PETER crosses the
road again and makes his way towards a tobacconist's. It is
next door but one to a photographer's – MORTIMER
BROWN Ltd. The photographer's window is crowded with
photographs, group photographs of wedding and local events,
photographs of good-looking children and grinning babies.
There is a notice in the window which reads: Anniversary
Exhibition 1945 – 1975.*

*As PETER passes the shop, he glances casually at the display
and proceeds towards the tobacconists. He is three or four
yards past the shop when he stops dead in his tracks, then
quickly returns to the photographer's window. He stands
staring at something in the window. We suddenly see what
has attracted his attention. In the window, next to a large
photograph of a wedding group, is a photograph of PHYLLIS
DU SALLE. PETER stares at the photograph in amazement,
then making a decision he goes into the shop.*

CUT TO: Inside MORTIMER BROWN's Shop. Day.
*PETER comes into the shop and moves to the counter.
Adjacent to the counter is a curtain behind which is the
photographic studio. The curtain is drawn back and
MORTIMER BROWN, the proprietor, comes into the shop.
He is a tall, thin, neatly dressed man, wearing glasses. He
greets PETER with what he hopes is a friendly smile.*

BROWN: Good morning.
PETER: Good morning. I've just been admiring your
           display.
BROWN: Thank you, sir. That's very kind of you. It's our
           Anniversary Exhibition. We've been established
           thirty years next month. Can I assist you in any
           way?

PETER: Er – yes, I think perhaps you can. A friend of
            mine is … getting married very shortly and he's
            asked me to arrange for the photographs.

BROWN: Is it a local wedding?

PETER: Yes … I suppose you'd call it local. Canford
            Cliffs.

BROWN: That's certainly within our area. We'd be
            delighted to help you. (*Picking up a brochure
            from the counter*) Perhaps you'd like to take one
            of our brochures.

PETER: Oh – thank you.

BROWN: That'll tell you everything you want to know. (*A
            smile*) Which is mainly the price, I imagine.

PETER: I don't think my friend will be too fussy about
            the price, providing the photographs are … what
            he wants …

BROWN: (*With a gesture towards the window*) I don't
            think he need worry about that, sir.

PETER: I … was particularly taken by the wedding group
            in the centre of the window.

*PETER moves to the window, indicating the photograph.
MORTIMER BROWN joins him, looking towards the
photograph.*

BROWN: Ah, yes! That's a wedding we covered in – when
            was it – July, I think. Rob Milton. He's the
            Chairman of the local Council. It was a dreadful
            day. Rained solidly the whole time. But you'd
            never think so, would you, from the
            photographs?

PETER: No, you certainly wouldn't. (*A moment, then
            casually indicating the photograph of PHYLLIS*)
            Do I recognise that girl? I seem to have seen her
            before somewhere.

BROWN: You could have seen her, sir. But not recently,
          I'm afraid. She and her husband were killed in an
          air crash about two years ago. A dreadful
          business.   Terribly sad. She was Sir Arnold
          Wyatt's daughter.

PETER stares at MORTIMER BROWN in stunned silence,
then slowly turning his head he looks down at the photograph.

END OF EPISODE ONE

EPISODE TWO

OPEN TO: Inside MORTIMER BROWN's Shop. Morning.

PETER is standing next to MORTIMER BROWN; both are near the shop window. PETER looks at BROWN for a moment, then slowly turning his head stares down at the photograph of PHYLLIS DU SALLE.

PETER: This … is a photograph of Sir Arnold Wyatt's daughter?

BROWN: Yes, that's right. I took it about a fortnight before the accident happened. (*Sadly; shaking his head*) Such a lovely girl. We were all deeply shocked when we heard that she and her husband had been killed.

The shop door opens, and a CUSTOMER enters. BROWN obviously recognises him.

BROWN: (*To CUSTOMER*) I'll be with you in a moment, sir.

CUSTOMER: Thank you.

BROWN: (*To PETER*) I think you'll find all the information you require in our brochure, sir.

PETER: (*Quietly; still obviously bewildered*) Thank you.

BROWN turns towards the customer.

CUT TO: Main Street of Heatherdown. Morning.

PETER comes out of the photographer's shop and moves to the edge of the pavement to cross the road. He hesitates, unable to resist looking back at the photographer's window; at the photograph of PHYLLIS DU SALLE. His expression is troubled as he crosses the road and goes into the café on the other side.

CUT TO: FLETCHER's CAFÉ: Heatherdown. Morning.

CLAUDE is seated at a table drinking a cup of coffee and glancing at a newspaper. He looks up and sees PETER approaching. He immediately realises that his brother has received a shock of some kind.

CLAUDE: What's the matter? You look as if you've seen a ghost!

PETER: I think I have!

PETER sits down and turning to a nearby waitress orders coffee.

PETER: There's a photographer's across the road. Mortimer Brown.

CLAUDE: Yes, I noticed it.

PETER: Did you look in the window?

CLAUDE: No, I didn't. Why?

PETER: If you had have done you'd have seen a photograph of Phyllis Du Salle.

CLAUDE: (*Softly*) Good God! Are you sure?

PETER: Absolutely sure. But that's only part of the story. I went into the shop and talked to Brown – at least, I assume it was Brown – and he told me it was a photograph of Sir Arnold Wyatt's daughter.

CLAUDE: But you told me about Wyatt's daughter. You said she'd been killed in an air crash, two years ago.

PETER: That's right. That's what Sir Arnold told me. The photograph in the window is a photograph of the girl I met in Geneva! The girl I brought down here three weeks ago! I'm absolutely sure of that.

CLAUDE: Then obviously Brown made a mistake. That's the only possible explanation.

PETER: Yes, but – he appeared to be in no doubt about it, Claude. As soon as I asked him about the photograph, he said it was Wyatt's daughter. He even mentioned her husband and talked about the accident.

58

A moment.

CLAUDE: Perhaps your friend Phyllis Du Salle just looks like the dead girl.

PETER: (*Shaking his head*) It was a photograph of Phyllis!

CLAUDE: Well, in that case, I think you ought to talk to Sir Arnold about this. I think you ought to tell him about the photograph and ask him if it is his daughter.

PETER: That could be difficult.

CLAUDE: Why difficult?

PETER: I've already called on him twice. I'm sure he thinks I'm a little – well, a little odd, to say the least.

CLAUDE: Well, I don't see what else you can do.

PETER nods. He looks distinctly puzzled.

A pause.

CLAUDE: (*After a slight hesitation*) Didn't you tell me he was a fan of mine?

PETER: Sir Arnold? Yes, he is.

CLAUDE: Then supposing you use me as an excuse and we both drop in on him?

PETER looks at CLAUDE; impressed by the suggestion.

PETER: Yes. Yes, I think that's a good idea. Thank you, Claude.

CLAUDE smiles at PETER.

CUT TO: Forest Gate Manor, Heatherdown. Morning.

PETER's car stops on the drive, outside the house. PETER and CLAUDE get out and go to the front door. PETER rings the doorbell. CLAUDE looks around interestedly as they wait.

CLAUDE: It's a lovely old building.

PETER: (*A shade tense*) Yes. Isn't it?

PETER rings again. A moment or two, then he hears someone coming to the door. They both look at the door as it opens. MRS CASSIDY appears. She is dressed for shopping and looks surprised on seeing PETER standing there.

PETER: (*Pleasantly*) Good morning, Mrs Cassidy. Do you think I might have a word with Sir Arnold?

MRS CASSIDY: I'm afraid he's rather busy at the moment, Mr Matty. But … (*Looking at CLAUDE*) I'll see what I can do.

PETER: Thank you.

As MRS CASSIDY turns away, we hear WYATT's voice from the background.

WYATT: (*Calling*) Who is it, Sheila?

MRS CASSIDY: It's Mr Matty!

WYATT arrives from the study.

PETER: I'm sorry to trouble you, Sir Arnold, but you did say …

WYATT: (*Looking at CLAUDE with obvious interest*) Not at all. Do come in, please!

PETER: Thank you …

WYATT: (*To MRS CASSIDY*) I'll meet you later, Sheila, in the village.

CUT TO: The Hall of Forest Gate Manor. Morning.

WYATT closes the front door as PETER and CLAUDE enter and MRS CASSIDY departs.

PETER: This is my brother – Claude. You said if he was ever in this part of the world …

WYATT: Yes! Yes, indeed! (*To CLAUDE*) I recognised you immediately, Mr Matty! This is a very pleasant surprise. I told your brother I very much hoped to have the pleasure of meeting you one day.

WYATT leads the way into the study.

CUT TO: The Study. Morning.
WYATT takes CLAUDE by the arm as the three men enter the study.

WYATT: You've given me so much pleasure, Mr Matty, over the years. I think I must have every recording you've ever made.

CLAUDE: Thank you, Sir Arnold. That's very nice to hear. I've just made a new one. I'll make sure my agent sends you a copy the moment it's released.

WYATT: That's most kind of you. I appreciate it.

CLAUDE looks at PETER.

PETER: (*Hesitant*) I hope you'll forgive me for intruding like this, but something happened this morning which, well …

WYATT: (*Pleasantly*) Go on, Mr Matty.

PETER: The last time I was here you told me about your daughter. You said both she and her husband were killed … in a plane crash …

WYATT: (*Puzzled*) Yes – that's right.

PETER: (*Not quite sure how to continue*) Well … I saw a photograph of your daughter this morning … At least, I was told it was your daughter …

CLAUDE: (*Coming to PETER's rescue*) Sir Arnold, did your daughter have her photograph taken by a man called Mortimer Brown?

WYATT: Yes, she did. I remember the day she went to him. As a matter of fact, it was my idea. I hadn't got a decent photograph of Pauline, and I thought … But – what's this all about? (*To PETER*) Why are you interested in my daughter, Mr Matty?

CLAUDE: My brother saw the photograph – it's in Mortimer Brown's window.

PETER: I thought it was a photograph of someone else, someone I know. So, I went into the shop and made inquiries about it. The photographer told me that … it was your daughter …

WYATT: In other words, you were mistaken?

PETER: I … don't know whether I was mistaken or not.

WYATT looks at CLAUDE, then at PETER again.

WYATT: I'm sorry, but I'm afraid I don't quite follow you?

CLAUDE: (*Quietly*) Could we possibly see a photograph of your daughter, sir?

WYATT: Yes, certainly! By all means …

WYATT crosses to an antique chest and opening one of the drawers takes out a large album. He opens the album as he rejoins CLAUDE and PETER.

WYATT: Is something wrong, Mr Matty?

PETER: That's … your daughter?

WYATT: Yes, of course!

CLAUDE: (*To PETER*) It's not Phyllis Du Salle?

PETER: (*Shaking his head*) No, it isn't! It definitely isn't!

WYATT: (*Perplexed*) Phyllis Du Salle?

PETER: The photograph in the window was a photograph of the woman I've been looking for – the one I told you about – Phyllis Du Salle.

WYATT: (*Staggered*) And Mortimer Brown told you it was my daughter?

PETER: Yes.

WYATT: But why on earth should he do that?

PETER: I can't imagine why.

PETER looks down at the album and the photograph of WYATT's daughter.

CUT TO: The Main Street of Heatherdown. Morning.

PETER's car draws up at the kerb and PETER gets out, followed by CLAUDE and WYATT. We are now aware that the car is parked outside of the photographer's shop. PETER looks at WYATT then points to a photograph in the shop window.

PETER: It's the one on the right, near the wedding group.

WYATT moves to the shop window and stares at the photograph. PETER and CLAUDE follow him to the window. PETER immediately reacts on seeing the photograph. We now see the photograph; it is similar to the one in Sir Arnold's album; the photograph of his daughter. WYATT looks at PETER.

WYATT: But this is my daughter! It's an enlargement of the photograph I've just shown you.

PETER: But … that wasn't the photograph I saw! The one I saw was … (*Almost lost for words*) quite different …

WYATT looks confused. So does CLAUDE. They exchange uneasy looks. PETER's face sets determinedly as he goes to the shop door.

CUT TO: Inside MORTIMER BROWN's shop. Morning.

The shop is empty. PETER enters and moves to the counter. After a momentary hesitation he raps on the counter. CLAUDE and WYATT enter the shop rather tentatively. MORTIMER BROWN comes through the curtained doorway leading to the back of the shop.

BROWN: Sorry to have kept you waiting, sir, but I was in the dark room. (*He appears not to have recognised PETER*) Can I help you?

PETER: I called earlier this morning and asked you about …

BROWN: Of course you did! I beg your pardon! It's
            coming into the light after being in there.
            (*Seeing WYATT and CLAUDE*) Oh – good
            morning, Sir Arnold!

WYATT: Good morning.

BROWN: I shan't keep you long, sir.

WYATT: That's all right. I'm with Mr Matty.

BROWN: Oh. Oh, I see. (*To PETER*) It was about a
            wedding, if I remember rightly?

PETER: Yes, but – that's not why I've called back.

BROWN: No?

WYATT: Mr Matty's still curious about the photograph of
            my daughter – the one in the window. I
            understand he's already spoken to you about it.

BROWN: (*Puzzled*) Yes, he has. (*To PETER*) What is it
            you want to know?

PETER: Well – in the first place I'd like to know why
            you've changed it?

BROWN: Changed it?

PETER: Yes.

BROWN: What do you mean, sir?

PETER: You know perfectly well what I mean. The
            photograph in the window isn't the same. It's not
            the one you showed me.

*BROWN looks at PETER somewhat taken aback by the
sudden sharpness in his voice.*

BROWN: I'm sorry, I don't quite understand. (*He crosses
            to the window*) I take it – you are referring to this
            photograph? (*He takes the photograph out of the
            window*)

PETER: No, I'm not! I'm referring to the photograph you
            showed me!

BROWN: But this is the one I showed you!

PETER: (*Shaking his head*) You showed me the photograph of a friend of mine – a Mrs Du Salle.

BROWN: Mrs Du Salle?

BROWN looks helplessly at CLAUDE, then at WYATT.

CLAUDE: Look, let's start at the beginning. My brother asked you about a photograph which was in your window.

BROWN: That's quite right, sir.

CLAUDE: He asked you who it was, and you said it was a photograph of Sir Arnold Wyatt's daughter.

BROWN: That's quite correct.

PETER: (*Pointing to the photograph in BROWN's hand*) Yes, but it wasn't that photograph!

BROWN: But it was, sir! Now I ask you, why on earth would I show you a photograph of someone else and pretend it was Sir Arnold's daughter?

PETER: (*Looking at BROWN*) I can't imagine why! But you did!

WYATT: (*Trying to be helpful*) Are you alone in the shop, Mr Brown? I mean – do you have an assistant?

BROWN: Yes, I do. A Mr Fellowes. I believe you've met him.

WYATT: Well, is it possible that Mr Fellowes could have changed the photograph without your knowing …

BROWN: (*Interrupting WYATT; obviously annoyed*) No, it isn't! He's away on holiday at the moment, besides … (*To PETER; adamant*) no one changed the photograph! This is the one you saw! The one I showed you! The one we talked about! Damn it all, it's been in the window the whole week!

BROWN is facing PETER as he speaks, holding up the photograph for him to see. WYATT looks at PETER.

65

CLAUDE is also looking at him. There is a pause, then without saying a word PETER slowly turns and walks out of the shop.

CUT TO: Main Street of Heathdown. Morning.

PETER comes out of MORTIMER BROWN's shop and crosses to his car. He looks tense and a shade annoyed as he lights a cigarette and stands waiting to be joined by WYATT and his brother. CLAUDE and WYATT emerge from the shop and cross to the car. They both appear to be a shade embarrassed by PETER's behaviour in the shop. PETER suddenly realises this.

PETER: I'm sorry if I embarrassed you.

WYATT: Er – not at all. In your place I'd have probably behaved in exactly the same way. But … obviously there must be a perfectly simple explanation.

PETER: There is a simple explanation! He's not telling the truth.

WYATT: But why should Mr Brown lie to you?

PETER: I don't know why.

CLAUDE: And why change the photograph in the window? After all, he didn't know you'd be coming back to the shop.

WYATT: That's true, Mr Matty.

PETER: In other words, you both think I made a mistake?

WYATT: (*After an awkward glance at CLAUDE*) Well – yes, to be perfectly honest, we do.

CLAUDE hesitates, then gives a nod of agreement.

PETER: Then there's nothing more to be said. (*Opening the car door*) If you jump in the car, Sir Arnold, I'll run you home.

WYATT: Thank you, Mr Matty, that won't be necessary. I have some business to attend to in the village.

           (*To   CLAUDE*) Goodbye, sir. It's been a great pleasure meeting you. I do hope we shall run across each other again sometime.

CLAUDE: I hope so too, Sir Arnold.

WYATT: (*To PETER; after a momentary hesitation*) Goodbye, Mr Matty.

PETER: Goodbye.

WYATT nods to CLAUDE and hurries away. CLAUDE makes to speak to PETER who is still holding the car door open, then changing his mind he gets into the JAGUAR. PETER closes the car door and goes round to the driving seat.

CUT TO: Inside PETER's Car. Morning.

PETER and CLAUDE are in the car. PETER looks thoughtful, CLAUDE distinctly worried. It is obvious that they have not spoken for some little time. PETER is driving and the car is slowing down at the entrance to the harbour.

PETER: I know what you're thinking, Claude.

CLAUDE: Do you, Peter?

PETER: You think I've been so obsessed with this girl that I imagined I saw her photograph in the window?

CLAUDE: I'm afraid you're wrong. That's not what I was thinking. But … it's a possibility, I suppose. A trick of the light … Perhaps that's what did happen.

PETER: (*Shaking his head*) Brown switched the photographs! Don't ask me why – but he switched them!

CLAUDE: (*Quietly*) I wish I could believe that.

PETER: (*Realising that his brother is concerned*) Then what do you think happened?

CLAUDE: I … don't know what happened, Peter. I just don't know.

PETER: (*A flicker of a smile*) Well, don't look like
                   that, old boy. I assure you, I'm not going
                   round the twist, if that's what you're
                   thinking. (*PETER brakes and the car pulls
                   up near the post office*) I've got to make a
                   phone call, Claude. I'll be back in five
                   minutes.

*When the car stops PETER jumps out of his seat and goes into
the post office. CLAUDE sits in the car, watching him. A
worried, concerned expression on his face.*

CUT TO: Inside the Post Office. Morning.

*MRS FRINTON is serving a customer. PETER is in the
telephone booth looking up a number in his pocketbook. The
door of the phone box is open. MRS FRINTON calls for
PETER as the customer leaves.*

MRS FRINTON: Thought your brother looked very well,
                   Mr Matty.

PETER: (*Dialling*) Yes, he's fine.

MRS FRINTON: How long is he staying down here?

PETER: Oh – probably a week or ten days. He
                   works very hard; he deserves a holiday.

MRS FRINTON: I'm sure he does. I only hope it keeps fine
                   for him. The weather report isn't too bad.

*As PETER completes his dialling, he closes the door of the
phone box. MRS FRINTON turns to serve another customer
who has just entered the shop. PETER, receiver to his ear,
listens to the number ringing out at the other end.*

PETER: (*Suddenly; on phone*) Hello! Is that you,
                   Max?

CUT TO: MAX LERNER's Flat. Islington. Day.

*MAX LERNER is on the telephone. We do not see a great deal
of the flat in this shot but enough to give us the impression of*

a small, vaguely untidy, bachelor flat belonging to a freelance journalist. For the duration of this conversation, we cut back and forth between MAX and PETER.

MAX: Oh, hello, Peter! How are things? Are you in Town?

PETER: No, I'm down at the coast. Max, I'd like to see you. I want to have a talk.

MAX: Yes, all right, Peter. Is it urgent?

PETER: Yes, it is rather. How are you placed at the moment?

MAX: Lots of lovely things in the offing, old boy. But as it happens, at this precise moment, I'm terrifyingly free.

PETER: Good. I'll see you this afternoon. Be at my flat at five o'clock.

MAX: (*Curious*) Yes, all right. But what's this all about?

PETER: I'll tell you when I see you.

MAX: No, I'm curious. Tell me now.

PETER: (*A moment, then:*) I'm offering you a job. An assignment.

MAX: A job?

PETER: Yes.

MAX: (*Delighted*) Five o'clock, old boy. On the dot.

CUT TO: Inside PETER's Car. Morning.

The car is stationary outside the village post office. CLAUDE, seated in the car, is looking thoughtfully ahead. He comes out of his thoughts with a start as the door opens and PETER gets into the car.

PETER: Sorry to have kept you waiting.

CLAUDE: That's all right.

PETER:	I'm afraid I've got to go back to London this afternoon. Something … rather important has cropped up.
CLAUDE:	Oh …
PETER:	Do you want to come back with me, or would you prefer to stay down here?
CLAUDE:	(*A moment; then:*) No, I'll stay on the boat if that's all right with you.
PETER:	Yes, of course. I'm sorry about this, Claude, but it is important.
CLAUDE:	Not to worry. After all, you mustn't neglect your business.

PETER looks at CLAUDE, his hand on the ignition key.

CUT TO:	The Hall of PETER's Flat. Day.

The front door opens. PETER enters and takes the key from the lock. He closes the front door and goes into the living room.

CUT TO: The Living Room of PETER's Flat. Day.

MRS GALLOWAY, PETER's daily help, is in the act of putting on her coat.

MRS GALLOWAY:	(*With a start; taken by surprise*) Oh, it's you, Mr Matty! Gave me quite a start!
PETER:	Sorry, Mrs Galloway. I didn't think you'd be here.
MRS GALLOWAY:	I'm a bit later than usual.

PETER crosses to his desk and takes a cheque book out of one of the drawers.

MRS GALLOWAY:	I thought you was staying on that boat of yours this weekend.
PETER:	(*Writing out a cheque*) I was – but I've got some business to attend to.

MRS GALLOWAY: Oh. Shame. Well, I'll be off then.

PETER: Yes. Thank you, Mrs Galloway. Have a nice weekend.

As MRS GALLOWAY goes out into the hall PETER tears the cheque out of the book and puts it in his pocket.

CUT TO: The Hall of PETER's Flat. Day.

MRS GALLOWAY opens the front door and is just about to leave when a somewhat breathless MAX LERNER arrives.

MAX: Is Mr Matty in?

MRS GALLOWAY: Yes, he's just this minute arrived. Who shall I say …

MAX: That's okay. He's expecting me.

MAX breezes past MRS GALLOWAY and enters the living room.

CUT TO: The Living Room of PETER's Flat. Day.

PETER turns towards the door as MAX enters.

MAX: Here we are, Squire! Five o'clock, on the dot!

PETER: Hello, Max! Good of you to come. Sit down. What would you like to drink?

MAX: What are you having?

PETER: Oh – I'll probably have a Scotch.

MAX: Same here.

PETER crosses to the drinks table. There is a slight pause during which PETER mixes the drinks. MAX watches him, trying to conceal his obvious curiosity.

PETER: Soda?

MAX: No – just a spot of water. (*Pause*) Where were you when you telephoned?

PETER: Poole. I drove back this afternoon.

MAX: Especially to see me?

71

PETER: (*Joining Max with the drinks*) Yes. I told you.
            I've got a job for you.
MAX: (*A sigh of relief*) Well, thank goodness for that. I
            thought perhaps you might have changed your
            mind while I was on my way over here. (*He
            takes the drink from PETER*)
PETER: Why should you think that?
MAX: Oh – no particular reason, but that's the sort of
            luck I've been having just lately. Frankly, I badly
            need work at the moment. All I can get.
PETER: Alimony troubles?
MAX: You've said it! My wives are at my throat again.
            All three of 'em.

*PETER takes the cheque from his pocket and hands it to
MAX.*

PETER: Well, maybe this will keep them quiet.

MAX looks at the cheque and is obviously delighted.

MAX: I say – that's pretty generous.
PETER: Don't worry, you're going to earn it. (*Raising his
            glass*) Skol!
MAX: Cheers.

A pause.

MAX: Well – what is this job?
PETER: Do you remember, about three or four weeks
            ago, I told you I'd met a girl called Phyllis Du
            Salle?
MAX: You met her on a plane coming back from
            Geneva.
PETER: That's right.
MAX: We talked about her husband – Norman. He was
            a journalist. He was killed, or rather lost his life,
            in an accident.
PETER: (*Nodding*) They were travelling from Marseilles
            to Corsica. Norman Du Salle went up on deck

72

one night and that was the last Phyllis saw of him.

MAX: I remember reading about it. (*A pause; then:*) Well – go on …

PETER: Phyllis told me about the accident. She also told me about the row she had with her husband the night he was drowned. It was about a doll.

MAX: Yes, I know. It was in the papers. (*A tiny pause*) Peter, get to the point. What is it you want me to do?

PETER: Phyllis Du Salle has disappeared.

MAX: (*Surprised*) Disappeared?

PETER: Yes – and I've got to find her. (*Tensely*) I've just got to find her!

MAX LERNER is looking at PETER.

MAX: You really have fallen for this girl, Peter, haven't you?

PETER: That's the understatement of the year! I'm crazy about her. I just can't get her out of my mind.

MAX: (*Shaking his head*) I've certainly never seen you like this before.

PETER: Max, I need help. You've just got to help me find her!

MAX: All right. All right, dear boy. (*Takes a notebook and pencil from his inside pocket*) This isn't exactly my line of country, but we'll see what we can do. Now how do I start?

PETER: Well, first of all, I'd like you to make some inquiries – discreet inquiries – about two men. Sir Arnold Wyatt and a man called Mortimer Brown. They both live in Heatherdown. Brown's a photographer, he has a shop in the High Street. Sir Arnold's a retired lawyer. He

	lives in a house called Forest Gate Manor, a very lovely house just outside the village.
MAX:	(*Writing down the names*) Sir Arnold Wyatt … Mortimer Brown. Okay. Now what is it you want to know about them?
PETER:	I want to know if, by any chance, they're close friends …

CUT TO:	Poole Harbour. Day.

CLAUDE, in old clothes, is vigorously swabbing the deck with a mop and a pail of water. He is obviously enjoying the physical exertion. He decides the water in the pail is dirty, empties it over the side and drops the pail, supported on a rope, into the sea. He is just in the act of hauling up the full pail when something arrests his attention. He looks towards the quayside. We follow his look to the person standing there on the quayside. It is SIR ARNOLD WYATT. He is holding something under his arm. An LP: a recording made by CLAUDE.

WYATT:	Good morning!
CLAUDE:	Oh, hello! Good morning!

WYATT smiles faintly at CLAUDE's surprise. He indicates the poised full pail of water on the rope in CLAUDE's hands.

WYATT:	Don't let me interrupt you!

CLAUDE smiles, hauls up the pail, and empties the contents back into the sea.

CLAUDE:	I'm glad you have! I think I'm in danger of overdoing it!
WYATT:	You're like me, I expect. Don't take any exercise for three or four months and then expect to make up for it in a couple of hours. May I come aboard?
CLAUDE:	Yes, of course. I'm sorry, I thought you were just passing.

74

WYATT climbs the gangplank onto the boat.

CLAUDE: My brother's in London, I'm afraid.

WYATT: It was you I wanted to see, Mr Matty. I was wondering if you'd be kind enough to autograph this LP for me. It's one of your recordings.

CLAUDE: Yes, of course.

WYATT: It's our Church fete next week and they're having an auction. They have one every year and I usually try to find something a little unusual for them.

CLAUDE: I'm afraid my pen's below, in my jacket. If you'll excuse me …

WYATT: (*Producing a ball pen*) No. No, here we are, Mr Matty.

CLAUDE: Oh – thank you.

CLAUDE takes the proffered pen and proceeds to write on the LP. A slight pause.

WYATT: (*Looking at what CLAUDE has written*) Oh – that's very nice. Most kind of you. (*He takes the record from CLAUDE*) Most kind. The vicar will be delighted with this, I'm sure.

CLAUDE hands back the pen.

CLAUDE: (*Making conversation*) Are you fond of sailing, Sir Arnold?

WYATT: No, I'm afraid not. I'm no sailor. I get bored so quickly, that's my trouble. Can't wait to get back to dry land and stretch my legs.

CLAUDE: Yes, I know what you mean. I must confess I enjoy it, but I'm afraid I get very little time for anything these days except work.

WYATT: Yes, I'm sure. I imagine you're both hard workers – both you and your brother.

CLAUDE: Yes, I suppose we are, really.

A pause.

75

WYATT: Your brother's in publishing, I believe?

CLAUDE: Yes, he is.

WYATT: Done awfully well, I hear. Only the other day someone was telling me his firm's got offices all over. Paris. Rome. New York.

CLAUDE: Well – Paris and New York certainly. I don't remember Peter saying anything about Rome.

WYATT: No? Well – I must have been mistaken. (*A moment, then:*) Your brother must travel a great deal, Mr Matty.

CLAUDE: (*Somewhat puzzled by this remark*) Yes, I suppose he does. But I'm the traveller, I'm afraid. I seem to live out of suitcases these days.

WYATT: Yes, of course. In your profession you would. Still, being a concert pianist must be very rewarding.

CLAUDE: (*Still a shade puzzled by the conversation*) It has its compensations, certainly.

WYATT: (*About to leave, then changing his mind*) Mr Matty, forgive me, but … your brother's called on me three times just recently and each time he's discussed a friend of his. A young lady called Mrs Du Salle.

CLAUDE: Yes, I know. And I think I know what you're thinking! And I can't honestly blame you! But I assure you, Mrs Du Salle does exist. She's not just a figment of my brother's imagination.

WYATT: Well, I'm relieved to hear you say so! I must confess I was beginning to wonder! (*Nodding at the LP*) Thank you again for this. Very kind of you. I appreciate it.

WYATT smiles at CLAUDE and moves to the gangplank. He waves goodbye as he finally goes off down the quay. CLAUDE watches him go, a faintly puzzled expression on his face. Thoughtfully, he picks up the rope and lets it slide through his fingers, lowering the pail into the sea. It falls into the water with a splash.

CUT TO: PETER MATTY's Office. Day.
PETER is at his desk looking through a file. MOLLIE enters from the outer office. She is carrying a letter.
MOLLIE: Here's the letter you're looking for.
PETER: Ah, thank you, Mollie.
MOLLIE: It was in the other file.
PETER: I knew I'd seen it somewhere recently.
AS MOLLIE moves to the door the telephone rings.
PETER: It's all right. I'll take it.
PETER picks up the receiver as MOLLIE continues out of the office.
PETER: Peter Matty speaking … Oh, it's you, Claude!

CUT TO: Inside the Village Post Office. Day.
CLAUDE is on the telephone in the phone box. MRS FRINTON is serving a little boy in the background. For the duration of this conversation, we cut back and forth between CLAUDE and PETER.
CLAUDE: Hello, Peter – how are you?
PETER: I'm all right, old boy. How are you making out? How's the boat?
CLAUDE: The boat's fine. I'm the one that's suffering. Too much hard work. When are you coming down here again?
PETER: Probably in a couple of days. I'm not sure.
CLAUDE: Well, try and make it for the weekend.
PETER: Oh, I'll be down for the weekend, definitely. If not before.
CLAUDE: I had a visit from a friend of yours this morning.

77

PETER: Oh? Who was that – Mrs Frinton?

CLAUDE: No, Sir Arnold Wyatt. He wanted me to autograph an LP – for charity. It's the Church fete and they're holding an auction.

PETER: Oh, I see. (*A moment*) What's the weather like down there?

CLAUDE: Not too bad. A bit windy. Are you busy?

PETER: Yes, we are at the moment.

CLAUDE: (*After a moment; curious*) By the way, Peter, have you people got an office in Rome?

PETER: (*Surprised by the question*) No. We have agents there, but we haven't got an office. We do very little business with Italy. But why this sudden interest in Matty Publications?

CLAUDE: Sir Arnold said someone told him you had an office in Rome, and I said I didn't think you had – that's all.

PETER: (*After a moment*) Did Sir Arnold say anything else?

CLAUDE: No, I don't think so. Nothing of importance. Although I must admit, I couldn't help feeling that the record was just an excuse …

PETER: An excuse for what?

CLAUDE: (*Puzzled*) I don't know. Let me know when you're coming down.

PETER: Yes, I will. I'll phone Mrs Frinton.

CLAUDE: Goodbye, Peter.

We stay in the village post office with CLAUDE as he replaces the receiver and emerges from the phone box. A new customer is now standing at the counter with his back towards CLAUDE.

CLAUDE: (*Thoughts elsewhere*) I'd like some cigarettes, Mrs Frinton.

MRS FRINTON:	Yes, o' course. Same sort as your brother?
CLAUDE:	Please.
MRS FRINTON:	I'll see if I've got some, dearie. But they're in short supply at the moment.

As MRS FRINTON disappears in search of the cigarettes the customer turns and looks at CLAUDE. CLAUDE immediately recognises him. It is MORTIMER BROWN.

BROWN:	(*Hesitant*) Mr Matty?
CLAUDE:	Yes …
BROWN:	I – I don't know whether you remember me, sir. Mortimer Brown. We met the other day when your brother …
CLAUDE:	Yes, of course I do!
BROWN:	I – I hope you'll excuse me, Mr Matty, but … I've been thinking about your brother, about the photograph, about what happened …
CLAUDE:	You're not the only one! I've been thinking about it too!
BROWN:	Yes! Yes, indeed. I'm sure you have! I had another chat with Sir Arnold – we bumped into each other yesterday afternoon. I'm afraid, like me, he's still utterly bewildered by the whole business.
CLAUDE:	So am I, Mr Brown. And so is my brother, if it comes to that. He just can't understand why the photograph was changed.
BROWN:	(*Adamant; but not unpleasant*) But it wasn't changed! I assure you it wasn't! The photograph you saw was the one in the window, the one I showed your brother in the first place.

CLAUDE looks at BROWN, but makes no comment.

BROWN: Mr Matty, I hope you'll forgive me asking this question but – has your brother been ill recently?

CLAUDE: He had laryngitis about six weeks ago.

BROWN: No. No, I didn't mean that. I meant, has your brother at any time … (*Hesitates*)

CLAUDE: Mr Brown, my brother isn't suffering from hallucinations, if that's what you're thinking. He's a perfectly sane, highly respectable businessman.

BROWN: (*Puzzled*) Yes. Yes, I know. That's what Sir Arnold told me. Then … how do you account for what happened?

CLAUDE: (*Still looking at BROWN*) I can't account for it.

BROWN: This woman – the person your brother's been looking for …?

CLAUDE: Mrs Du Salle.

BROWN: Yes. Have you seen her?

CLAUDE: Yes, but only briefly. I caught a glimpse of her at Geneva Airport. I certainly wouldn't recognise her again.

BROWN: <u>But you have actually seen her?</u>

CLAUDE: (*Quietly*) Yes, I've seen her.

MRS FRINTON returns with the cigarettes.

MRS FRINTON: Here we are, Mr Matty. That'll be thirty-five p.

CLAUDE: Thank you, Mrs Frinton.

CLAUDE takes the packet of cigarettes and gives MRS FRINTON the money. He looks at BROWN again, hesitates as if about to say something, then with a brief nod, crosses towards the door.

CUT TO: PETER MATTY's Office. Day.

It is late afternoon. PETER is seated at his desk critically examining a number of book jacket designs. MOLLIE enters carrying documents. She is in a hurry to get away and glances at her watch as she puts the papers down on PETER's desk.

MOLLIE: Do you want these to go off tonight?

PETER: I don't really know until I've looked at them. Why?

MOLLIE: I did say I'd like to get away early today.

PETER: Yes, of course you did! I'm sorry, Mollie. Off you go. If there's anything urgent, I'll post it myself.

MOLLIE: Thanks, Mr Matty.

As MOLLIE moves to the door PETER picks up the papers she has left on the desk. MOLLIE suddenly remembers something.

MOLLIE: Oh, I forgot to tell you. Max Lerner phoned while you were out at lunch.

PETER: Max? What did he want?

MOLLIE: He'd like you to call round and see him sometime this evening.

PETER: What time?

MOLLIE: He said any time after five o'clock.

PETER: I see. Did he say anything else?

MOLLIE: No, that's all. He sounded a little … embarrassed, I thought.

PETER: (*Looking at MOLLIE*) Thank you, Mollie. See you tomorrow.

MOLLIE hurries out, closing the door behind her. PETER picks up the documents, looks at them, hesitates, then he suddenly rises and crosses towards the door.

CUT TO: A block of flats in Islington. Late Afternoon.

The entrance to a block of flats in Islington. A rather dismal area. The distant sound of harsh music coming from a nearby pub; the kind that provides entertainment.

The Jaguar draws up outside the entrance to the block of flats and PETER gets out. He stands there for a moment, reacting to the seediness of the surroundings, then finally goes into the entrance to the block of flats.

CUT TO: The entrance of the block of flats. Late Afternoon.

PETER goes to the bell buttons and entrance phone. We see the button with the name MAX LERNER alongside it. PETER presses the button. PETER waits to hear MAX's voice in reply. He waits in vain. He presses the button once more. And again there is no reply from MAX. He presses it again. No reply. PETER looks slightly perplexed. He shrugs, moves to the staircase and ascends the stairs.

CUT TO: A corridor. Late afternoon.

This is a corridor on the first floor of the block of flats.

PETER ascends the last few stairs leading to the corridor. He stands there wondering which of the three doors is MAX LERNER's. He walks past the first one, stops at the second and looks at the number on the door and the ornamental door-knocker. He is about to use the knocker when he notices something. The door is ajar. PETER pushes it open, and walks into the flat.

CUT TO: MAX LERNER's Flat. Late Afternoon.

PETER enters the small hall of the flat, calling as he does so.

PETER: Max!

There is no reply. PETER carries on into the living room. He stands there looking around the rather untidy, book-littered room. He sees another door at the far end of the room; the

82

door leading to the kitchenette. He moves to the door, calling again:

PETER: Max!

No reply. PETER, faintly puzzled, turns back into the room. He looks at his watch, wondering whether to wait or not. There is a sound outside. PETER looks towards the door leading to the hall. The front door is heard closing and a moment later MAX LERNER enters. He is carrying a bottle of milk. He is astonished to find PETER facing him.

MAX: Peter! My goodness, you made me jump!

PETER: Isn't it a little unwise to leave the front door open?

MAX: Yes, but I just popped upstairs. Can't stand black coffee. (*Indicating the bottle of milk*) Had to borrow this from the young lady in the flat above. I'm always borrowing something off her. Have to cut it out. She's beginning to think I fancy her.

MAX grins a shade self-consciously.

PETER: My secretary said you wanted to see me.

MAX nods.

MAX: That's right. (*Obviously somewhat ill at ease*) Will you have some coffee?

PETER: Yes – thanks.

MAX seems glad of the excuse to hurry away into the kitchenette. PETER stands there, rather puzzled by MAX's seeming inability to look him in the eye.

MAX: (*Calling*) Do you take sugar?

PETER: Just one, please.

PETER moves to the doorway of the kitchenette watching MAX as he pours the water from the kettle into two brightly coloured mugs.

PETER: Mollie didn't tell me you'd phoned until half an hour ago, otherwise I'd have called you back.

MAX: Not to worry.

Max hands PETER one of the mugs.

83

PETER: Thanks.

MAX picks up his own mug of coffee, spills it slightly and curses under his breath. He comes out of the kitchenette nervously aware of PETER's gaze.

MAX: I don't charge for seats, you know.

PETER sits. MAX sits opposite him but slightly away in order not to face him.

PETER: (*Quietly*) Well? Why don't you tell me and get it over with?

MAX hesitates, finally looking at PETER.

PETER: Look, Max. I asked you to make certain inquiries for me. If you've found out something unpleasant, something you think I don't want to hear about – that's my problem. Not yours.

MAX: It isn't that.

PETER: Well, there's certainly something on your mind. Go ahead! Let's have it!

A pause.

MAX continues looking at PETER, finally he starts to say something, then changes his mind. Then he puts down his mug of coffee, takes something out of his pocket and hands it to PETER.

PETER: This is the cheque I gave you.

MAX: That's right. I'm giving it back to you.

PETER: Giving it back?

MAX: Yes. I'm sorry, Peter, but I can't accept the job you offered me.

PETER: But you have accepted it.

MAX: Then I've changed my mind.

PETER stares at MAX.

PETER: Why? Why have you changed your mind? (*Pause*) You said you needed a job. You told me you badly needed money.

84

MAX: Yes, I know I did, Peter, but … that was before I had this fantastic offer.

PETER: What offer?

MAX: There's a new advertising agency opening up. They're going to make films, advertising films, for television. They've … Well – they've offered me a five-year contract.

PETER: I see.

MAX: (*Not very convincing*) I was in television originally, you know. I've always wanted to get back. (*He waits for PETER to comment*) This offer's so good, so incredibly good, I … just can't turn it down. Honestly, old boy, I really can't.

PETER: When are you due to start?

MAX: The end of next week. I'm flying out to Stockholm at the weekend.

PETER: Stockholm?

MAX: Yes, it's an American company but they're based in Stockholm.

PETER: How did you hear of this offer?

MAX: I … answered an advertisement about six weeks ago. I forgot all about it and then suddenly, out of the blue, they telephoned me.

PETER: When?

MAX: When?

PETER: Yes. When did they telephone you?

MAX: Oh. On Tuesday night … or was it Wednesday? I'm not really sure. Look, I'm awfully sorry about this, I really am. I hate letting you down. I hate letting anyone down, but … I really have no alternative.

PETER: Supposing I make this proposition of mine worthwhile? I mean – really worthwhile.

MAX: What do you mean?

PETER: I don't know what these people are offering you, but – just suppose I double it. What then?

MAX: It – it wouldn't work. It's frightfully generous of you. Bloody generous, in fact, but … it just wouldn't work.

PETER: Why not?

MAX: I've told you. I want to get back into television. Besides, I've got problems here, in London. Three ex-wives. Alimony. God knows what! The thought of getting away, living in another country, appeals to me right now.

PETER: (*Trying to conceal his annoyance*) Yes, all right, Max. Forget it. There's nothing more to be said. (*Puts down his drink*) Thanks for the cheque. And the coffee.

PETER moves to the door.

MAX: (*Quietly; not looking at PETER*) Peter, please don't think I'm ungrateful. Please don't think I've forgotten all you've done for me in the past. You've been a damn good friend in more ways than one. I shall always … try and remember that.

PETER: (*A shade puzzled*) Thank you, Max.

PETER goes.

CUT TO: Block of Flats. Entrance. Late Afternoon.

PETER moves to his parked car, taking the car keys out of his pocket. As he unlocks the car door something attracts his attention. We see what it is. A plastic envelope is tucked under his windscreen wiper. PETER picks up the envelope and stares in the direction of the traffic warden who is just walking away further down the road. PETER shakes his head with irritation as he unlocks his car door.

CUT TO: PETER MATTY's Flat. Late afternoon.

PETER enters in his outdoor clothes. He looks depressed and a shade angry as he takes off his coat, flings it onto a chair, and gets himself a drink. He then flops into an armchair and takes the plastic envelope from his pocket together with the cheque MAX LERNER returned to him.

PETER shakes his head with annoyance as he tears up the cheque and drops it into the nearby waste-paper basket. He sips his drink and looks sullenly at the plastic envelope on his lap. He opens the envelope and takes out the summons.

A slip of paper falls into his lap. PETER picks up the slip of paper, unfolds it, and reads what is written on it. He stares at the piece of paper, the shock of the words causing him to rise involuntarily from the chair. The 'summons' has fallen from his hand, totally forgotten.

We see the message typed on the slip of paper in PETER's hand. It reads:

"Mrs Du Salle has an appointment with her dentist at four o'clock tomorrow afternoon – 28A Harley Street."

CUT TO: Harley Street. London. Day.

PETER is searching for Number 28A. He continues down the street. He suddenly realises that he has arrived at the house he is looking for. He consults the names on the highly polished brass plate by the side of the door. We see the name: BASIL J. REED, Dental Surgeon. PETER goes to the front door and rings the doorbell. After a moment a uniformed RECEPTIONIST opens the door.

RECEPTIONIST: Good afternoon. Can I help you?

PETER: I – I believe a friend of mine has an appointment with Mr Reed at four o'clock.

RECEPTIONIST: Four o'clock?

PETER: That's right. Mrs Du Salle.

87

RECEPTIONIST: Ah, yes, of course. Mrs Du Salle's appointment should have been at four, but it was changed to three-thirty. You've just missed her, I'm afraid.

PETER: Oh …

The RECEPTIONIST smiles at PETER and closes the door. PETER turns disconsolately away and walks down the street. As he reaches a zebra crossing, a sudden thought occurs to him and he stands deep in thought. Finally, he makes a decision. He has made up his mind to return to the house and question the receptionist. At this moment a taxi turns the corner and slows down as it approaches the pedestrian crossing. PETER glances idly at the driver and then at the sole occupant of the cab. To his utter amazement he realises that he is staring at <u>PHYLLIS DU SALLE</u>.

The taxi gathers speed, leaving PETER on the pavement, dumbfounded, staring after it.

The taxi suddenly stops, along with the traffic which is drawn up at the traffic lights about thirty yards further on.

PETER immediately comes to life again and races down the road. Just as the lights change and the taxi draws away PETER flings open the taxi door and jumps inside.

CUT TO: Inside the Taxi. Day.

A shocked PHYLLIS is staring at PETER as he moves towards her.

PETER: Phyllis! Where the hell have you been? I've been looking all over for you!

PHYLLIS simply stares at PETER in alarm and disbelief.

PETER: Why didn't you come back to the boat? Did I offend you? Didn't you want to see me again?

PHYLLIS: (*Interrupting PETER*) No! No! I wanted to see you again! I intended to come back but

88

	… (*Tensely; frightened*) Peter, please leave me alone! Please go!
PETER:	(*Shaking his head; taking hold of her arm*) You've got to tell me what this is all about! I want to know why you lied to me! Why you suddenly disappeared! Why you decided to …
PHYLLIS:	Peter, please! Leave me alone!
PETER:	Don't you realise what I've been through during the past weeks! Every day – every single day – I've thought about you! There hasn't been a moment when you haven't occupied my thoughts …

At this moment the taxi driver pulls the cab to a sudden standstill and PETER falls backwards. PHYLLIS quickly opens the door on her side of the cab.

PETER:	(*Trying to restrain PHYLLIS from getting out*) Phyllis, listen to me! You've got to listen to me!
PHYLLIS:	(*Desperately*) Let go of my arm!
PETER:	Not until you've told me what this is all about!
PHYLLIS:	I can't! I can't tell you! Peter, please leave me alone!
TAXI DRIVER:	Do as she says, mate!

PETER looks at the angry TAXI DRIVER who is standing on the kerb and has wrenched the taxi door open. PETER instinctively releases his hold on PHYLLIS and before he can stop her, she jumps out of the taxi and runs off down the pavement.

PETER:	(*Jumping out of the cab*) Phyllis!

PETER makes to move after PHYLLIS, but the TAXI DRIVER quickly grabs hold of his jacket.

89

PETER: Look – you stay out of this! It's none of
                your business!
TAXI DRIVER: What goes on in my taxi, mate, is very
                much my business!
PETER: Kindly let go of me!

*With this remark PETER tears himself violently out of the
man's grasp. The TAXI DRIVER, incensed by this, aims a
blow at PETER. PETER half evades the blow, but it catches
him on the shoulder, and he falls partly against the taxi. He
now sees something on the floor. It is PHYLLIS's handbag.
He picks it up.*

TAXI DRIVER: Oh, no, you don't!

The TAXI DRIVER makes to wrest the handbag from PETER.

PETER: Don't be an idiot! She's a friend of mine!
TAXI DRIVER: Friend! God 'elp your enemies!

*PETER partly pushes the man aside and attempts to escape.
The TAXI DRIVER quickly, and angrily, reacts to this –
pulling PETER around and striking him in the face. A small
crowd of onlookers, including two excitable women, have
gathered by this time and they watch excitedly as PETER
wrestles with the TAXI DRIVER for possession of the
handbag. Cars have stopped to watch 'the fun', consequently
traffic is being held up and horns are starting to sound
furiously. PETER and the TAXI DRIVER struggle breathlessly
on.*

PETER: Look, I'm warning you …
TAXI DRIVER: That handbag was left in my cab and I'm
                responsible for it …

*With an aggressive movement, PETER flings the TAXI
DRIVER away from him and the man goes headlong into the
gutter. PETER pushes his way through the crowd, his eyes
searching frantically for a sign of PHYLLIS.*

*He runs the short distance to the nearest corner. In turning it
he collides with two POLICEMEN who, hearing the*

commotion, are hurrying to the scene of what they believe to be an accident.
PETER makes to sidestep but the POLICEMEN bar his path, their eyes immediately taking in the handbag. PETER suddenly realises what they are staring at and he too looks down at the handbag he is holding.

CUT TO: The Reception Desk at the local Police Station. Day.
PETER, the TAXI DRIVER, and the two WOMEN who witnessed the struggle on the pavement are facing the DESK SERGEANT. The POLICEMAN who arrested PETER stands nearby. Both the witnesses and the TAXI DRIVER are talking at once and the DESK SERGEANT is a little tired of their behaviour.

1st WOMAN: It's no use telling me what happened! I know what happened! I know what happened, I saw it with my own eyes …

SERGEANT: Madam, will you please be quiet! I can't get a word in edgeways.

There is silence. They all look at the DESK SERGEANT who turns towards PETER.

SERGEANT: You say you knew the lady, sir?

PETER: Yes. I've already told you that. She was a friend of mine.

SERGEANT: Was a friend of yours?

PETER: I use the past tense simply because I … haven't seen her for some time and she … disappeared with my car.

SERGEANT: (*This is beginning to make sense at last*) Oh, I see! So she stole your car, sir.

PETER: No. No, not exactly. I – I lent it to her.

SERGEANT: You lent it to her, and she didn't return it?

91

PETER:	Yes. Er – no! No, she returned it, but … Look, Sergeant, I think we'd better forget the car.
SERGEANT:	Yes, I think perhaps we'd better, sir. Tell me about the handbag.
PETER:	There's nothing to tell. My friend dropped it and I picked it up.
2nd WOMAN:	That's not true! He snatched it from her! I saw him do it!
PETER:	Madam, you saw nothing of the kind!
1st WOMAN:	Yes, she did! We both saw you!
2nd WOMAN:	You snatched it from her just as she was running away from the taxi.
PETER:	That's not true! I simply picked it up! (*To the TAXI DRIVER*) You know damn well I picked it up! You saw me do it.

The SERGEANT looks at the TAXI DRIVER for confirmation.

TAXI DRIVER:	Yes, he picked it up. 'Course he picked it up! But what the 'ell does that prove? He probably dropped it in the first place!
SERGEANT:	Was the handbag in his hand when you opened the taxi door?
TAXI DRIVER:	(*With a look at PETER*) I don't know. I'm not sure.
2nd WOMAN:	Yes, it was! I saw it! (*To the other WOMAN*) We both saw it! It was in his hand.
1st WOMAN:	That's right.

The SERGEANT looks at PETER again, then opens a large book and picks up a pen.

SERGEANT:	What do they call this friend of yours, sir?
PETER:	Mrs Du Salle …
SERGEANT:	And her address?

PETER: (*Both despondent and exasperated*) I don't
              know her address!
SERGEANT: You ... don't know her address?
PETER: No, I don't!
SERGEANT: Has she a telephone number?
PETER: I don't know whether ... (*He indicates the
              handbag on the counter before the
              SERGEANT*) I suggest you look in the
              handbag.
POLICEMAN: I've already looked, Sergeant. There's no
              means of identification.
The SERGEANT nods.
SERGEANT: (*To PETER*) I'm afraid I shall have to book
              you, sir.
PETER: Not before I've spoken to my solicitor.
SERGEANT: Name, please?
PETER: I insist on telephoning my solicitor.
SERGEANT: All in good time, sir. Now if you'll kindly
              give me your name.
PETER glares at the TWO WOMEN.
PETER: Matty.
SERGEANT: How do you spell that?
PETER: M.A.T.T.Y ...
SERGEANT: Initials?
PETER: P. Peter Matty.
SERGEANT: (*To the POLICEMAN*) What time did you
              pick him up?
POLICEMAN: Five minutes past four.
*The telephone rings and the SERGEANT puts down his pen
and picks up the receiver.*
SERGEANT: (*On the phone*) Sergeant Clifford ... Yes,
              that's right. Who is that speaking? (*A distinct
              note of deference enters his voice*) Yes, sir ...
              Yes, sir, I'm listening ...

They all watch the SERGEANT as he listens attentively to the man's voice on the other end of the line.

SERGEANT: Yes, he is … (*He looks at PETER*) I understand perfectly, sir … Yes, of course … Not a word, sir … Very good, sir.

The SERGEANT replaces the receiver, comes around the counter and opens a door leading to another office.

SERGEANT: (*To the TAXI DRIVER and the two witnesses*) If you'll step in here for a moment, please. No – not you, Mr Matty.

Rather mystified, PETER stands aside while the TAXI DRIVER and the two witnesses are ushered into the office. The SERGEANT gives a meaning little nod to the POLICEMAN who immediately joins them. The SERGEANT closes the office door and returns to PETER.

SERGEANT: Mr Matty …

PETER: Yes?

SERGEANT: You're free to go.

PETER stares at the SERGEANT in amazement.

PETER: Free to go?

SERGEANT: Yes, that's right. There'll be no charge. You're dismissed.

Without looking at PETER the SERGEANT returns to his place behind the counter and closes his book.

CUT TO: MOLLIE STAFFORD's Office. Morning.

MOLLIE is at her desk when PETER enters. He wears outdoor clothes, carries a morning newspaper, and looks like a man who has had a somewhat disturbed night.

MOLLIE: Good morning, Mr Matty. The post was early this morning. It's on your desk. There's quite a collection.

PETER: (*Absently*) Oh – thank you.

94

MOLLIE: There's a letter from Angela Blackwood. She's finished her novel at long last! (*Shaking her head*) One book every four years. I don't know how on earth she manages to live!

PETER: I do. She has a fleet of wealthy boyfriends.

MOLLIE: You must be joking! She looks like a horse …

PETER gives a faint smile and goes into his office.

CUT TO: PETER MATTY's Office. Morning.

PETER puts down his newspapers, takes off his coat, and after hanging it in a cupboard half-heartedly turns his attention to the pile of letters on his desk. The telephone tinkles and after glancing at this he continues to read his mail. After a moment he takes his usual place behind his desk and, opening one of the drawers, takes out a large folder. He is studying the papers in the folder when MOLLIE enters.

MOLLIE: Excuse me. There's a gentleman on the phone. He won't give his name, but he insists on speaking to you.

PETER: (*Shaking his head*) Find out what he wants.

MOLLIE: I've asked him. He won't tell me. But he's very polite. (*Smiling*) Got rather a nice voice.

PETER: Tell him I can't speak to him until I know what it's about.

MOLLIE: (*Hesitating*) Yes, all right.

MOLLIE goes out and PETER continues reading his papers.
A pause.
MOLLIE returns.

MOLLIE: I've spoken to him. He says it's a personal matter – about a friend of yours.

PETER: A friend of mine? (*He looks at MOLLIE for a moment*) All right – put him on.

MOLLIE goes out. PETER looks at the phone on his desk, obviously curious. As the phone tinkles he picks up the

95

receiver. There is no intercutting during this phone call. We
merely hear the voices at the other end.

PETER: (*On the phone*) Peter Matty speaking …
OSBORNE: (*An   attractive,   well-modulated   voice,*
                indicative of an easy manner) Mr Matty, I'm
                sorry to trouble you so early in the morning
                …
PETER: (*Interrupting OSBORNE*) Who are you? Who
                is it speaking?
OSBORNE: We have a mutual friend – Mrs Du Salle –
                and she's asked me to telephone you and say,
                first of all, how very sorry she is about the
                incident which occurred yesterday. And
                secondly …
PETER: (*A shade irritated*) Look, Mr-whatever-your-
                name-is, if Mrs Du Salle has a message for
                me, I'd like her to deliver it personally.
OSBORNE: (*Pleasantly*) Do you know, I thought you'd
                say that! And I must confess it's a point of
                view with which I have the utmost sympathy.
                If you hold on, Mr Matty, I'll see what I can
                do for you.

A pause.
PETER looks at the phone, puzzled, wondering whether he
will ever hear from the stranger again. Suddenly he hears
another, and more familiar voice.

PHYLLIS: Peter – it's Phyllis.
PETER: Where are you? Where are you speaking from
                – and who was that on the phone just now?
PHYLLIS: (*Calmly; with no trace whatever of emotion in*
                her voice) Peter, please listen to me. I'm sorry
                about yesterday. I lost my head. I shouldn't
                have disappeared like that …
PETER: (*Wryly*) You seem to make a habit of it.

PHYLLIS: I made a mistake in the first place, in letting you drive me down to Dorset that day. I've regretted it ever since. I apologise for all the trouble I've caused you.

PETER: Look – we can't talk on the phone! I've got to see you! I've a hundred and one questions I want to ask you.

PHYLLIS: (*Almost business-like; no emotion*) I'm sorry, I can't see you. It's quite out of the question.

PETER: Why is it out of the question?

PHYLLIS: (*Firmly*) I've just told you. I made a mistake, and I don't want to see you again. I'm sorry, but … that's the way it is.

PETER: (*Softly; almost stunned*) Is that … really what you want?

PHYLLIS: Yes. I don't want to sound offensive, but … there's just no point in our meeting again. I should only regret it.

PETER: (*Puzzled; obviously hurt*) Have I annoyed you? Have I offended you in any way?

PHYLLIS: No. Not at all.

PETER: Then why …

PHYLLIS: I just don't want to see you again. It's as simple as that.

PETER: (*Suddenly; angry*) Yes, well it's not as simple as that so far as I'm concerned! I want to see you! I want to know why you lied to me! Why you told me that story about Sir Arnold Wyatt! Why you deliberately … (*He breaks off as he suddenly hears the dialling tone; PHYLLIS has obviously rung off*)

PETER sits staring at the receiver in his hand.

CUT TO: The Saloon Bar of The Blue Boar. Evening.

The Blue Boar is a typical Bloomsbury pub. It is early evening, and the saloon bar is virtually deserted except for PETER and JULIAN OSBORNE, a distinguished looking man in his early forties. Both men are sitting at the bar several stools apart from each other. There is a telephone on the shelf at the back of the bar.

DON, the barman, looks a shade perturbed and the reason is obvious. PETER – one of DON's highly respected regulars – has already had too much to drink. OSBORNE is reading a newspaper and appears totally unaware of PETER's existence.

PETER: I'll have another one, Don.

DON: Er – yes, sir.

PETER: The same again.

DON: Yes, sir.

PETER: Is that … Is that three I've had?

DON: Four, sir.

PETER: Four? Are you sure?

DON: Yes. Four doubles, Mr Matty. (*Hesitating*) Are you sure you'd like another one, sir?

PETER: I'm positive.

DON: It's none of my business, Mr Matty, but – are you driving, sir?

PETER: No, I'm not driving. And you're quite right. (*Spelling it out*) It – is – none – of – your – business.

DON: I'm sorry, sir.

DON starts to get PETER his drink.

PETER: (*Relenting*) That's all right. No hard feelings. Perhaps you'll join me?

DON: That's very kind of you, sir, but not at the moment.

A slight pause.

PETER:	Are you a married man, Don?
DON:	Yes, sir. I'm afraid I am.
PETER:	Don't be afraid; I'm glad to hear it. (*Raising his glass*) Because this is what happens to a bachelor when he makes a bloody fool of himself.
DON:	Well – not to worry, sir. It happens to all of us, at one time or another.

DON puts the fresh drink down on the bar and as he does so the phone rings.

DON:	Excuse me. (*He turns and picks up the phone*) Hello? … Yes, it is … Who did you say? … Yes, he's right here … (*To OSBORNE*) It's for you, sir.
OSBORNE:	Oh. Is there a box?
DON:	No, I'm sorry. I'm afraid you'll have to take it here, sir. (*He lifts the phone and puts it down in front of OSBORNE*)
OSBORNE:	Thank you. (*He partly turns his back on PETER and DON as he picks up the receiver*) Hello? … (*Recognising the voice*) Oh, hello! … Where are you, where are you speaking from? … Yes, of course I'm listening … Are you sure? Are you sure it's our friend? … you recognised him? … Is he still in the flat? … I see … No, don't do that, stick to our arrangements … I'll meet you in about fifteen minutes.

OSBORNE replaces the receiver and DON, somewhat puzzled by what he has heard, removes the telephone back to its original position.

OSBORNE:	(*After a moment, to DON*) How much do I owe you?
DON:	Let me see – that'll be exactly 40p, sir.

OSBORNE: (*Handing DON 50p*) Keep the change.
DON: Thank you, sir.
OSBORNE: Good night.
DON: Good night, sir. Thank you.

OSBORNE picks up his hat and coat from a nearby stool and moves towards the exit; as he reaches PETER, he stops and for the first time looks at him.

OSBORNE: (*Pleasantly*) I shouldn't stay here too long, Mr Matty. I'm afraid you have rather a busy evening ahead of you.

OSBORNE leaves. PETER stares after him, taken aback by his statement.

CUT TO: A London Street. Outside of PETER's Flat. Evening.

A taxi draws up to the house and PETER gets out and starts to fumble in his pockets for the necessary change. He finally discovers the amount he requires and after paying the driver he crosses towards the front door of the house. The taxi pulls away from the kerb and as it does so a sports car races round the corner, narrowly missing the cab, and disappearing into the distance. PETER hears the roar of the sports car and turning catches a brief glimpse of the driver. The man at the wheel looks remarkably like MAX LERNER.

CUT TO: The Living Room of PETER's flat. Evening.

PETER enters the flat; starts to take off his coat, then stops dead! He stares at the ransacked room in utter astonishment. Someone has quite ruthlessly searched the room from top to bottom. Drawers have been opened and the contents scattered; cupboards have been ransacked; the drinks cabinet searched; bookshelves torn from the walls. PETER stands transfixed, then quickly pulling himself together he rushes into the bedroom.

CUT TO: PETER's Bedroom. Evening.
The bedroom has received precisely the same treatment as the living room. Even the bed has been stripped and the mattress ripped open. PETER stands in the doorway staring in anger and bewilderment at the scattered contents of his wardrobe.

CUT TO: The Living Room of MAX LERNER's Flat. Night.
JUDY LANGHAM is sprawled on the settee reading a magazine and sipping a gin and tonic. She is a hard, extremely sexy girl, and at this precise moment she is obviously irritated at being kept waiting. As she glances at her watch the door bursts open, and MAX enters. He looks both tired and agitated as he peels off his driving gloves.

JUDY: (*Rising*) Where the hell have you been?

MAX: I had an appointment.

JUDY: You're dead right! You had an appointment with me! You said seven o'clock.

MAX: (*Angry; turning on JUDY*) I know what I said! (*Dropping his gloves onto a chair*) How long have you been here?

JUDY: I've just told you! Since seven ...

MAX: Has anyone telephoned?

JUDY: No. Look, I'm supposed to be seeing another friend of mine at half-past nine ...

MAX: Shut up! (*He crosses to the phone and quickly dials a number*)

JUDY: If that's the sort of mood you're in you can get stuffed! I didn't come here to ...

MAX: Judy, for God's sake shut up!

We hear the number ringing out. MAX speaks immediately the receiver is lifted at the other end.

MAX: (*On the phone*) This is Max! Listen – let me do the talking! It didn't work! I searched the flat from top

101

to bottom and I didn't find a God-damned-thing! On top of which I think he saw me …

There is a sudden knock on the front door and Max quickly puts the phone down and turns towards the hall. The knock is repeated.

JUDY: (*Anxiously*) Who is it?

MAX: (*A sudden decision*) Go in the bedroom and take your clothes off.

JUDY: (*Taken aback*) What?

MAX: For God's sake, Judy – do as I tell you! Go in the bedroom and take your clothes off!

JUDY hesitates, then quickly goes into the bedroom. MAX picks up his gloves and follows her.

CUT TO: The Front Door of MAX LERNER's Flat. Night.

An agitated looking PETER is standing at the door, his hand on the door knocker. He knocks. A pause. He knocks again. A pause. He is about to use the knocker again when we hear MAX's voice calling from inside the flat.

MAX: (*Angry*) Who is it?

PETER: (*Calling back*) It's Peter! Peter Matty! I want to talk to you.

A pause. The door opens. Max appears wearing a dressing gown and quite obviously very little else.

MAX: Hello, Peter. What are you doing here?

PETER brushes past him into the hall, MAX follows.

PETER: (*Turning; facing MAX*) Did you go to my flat this evening?

MAX: Your flat?

PETER: Yes.

MAX: No. Why? You look devilishly agitated, Squire. What is it?

PETER: If you didn't go to my flat what were you doing in Lenton Street?

MAX: (*Apparently puzzled*) In Lenton Street?
PETER: Yes.
MAX: When was I in Lenton Street?
PETER: About half an hour ago. I saw you. You were in
           your car.
MAX: (*Shaking his head*) Not me! I've been here the
           whole afternoon. I took a friend out to lunch and
           we've er ... been here ever since. But what the
           devil is this all about? Why the excitement?
PETER: Someone broke into my flat! They ransacked the
           place; searched it from top to bottom.
MAX: Jeez! I'm sorry to hear that. But I fail to see what
           on earth it's got to do with ... Good God, you
           surely don't think I was responsible!
PETER: (*Facing MAX; bluntly*) Were you?
MAX: (*Apparently extremely annoyed*) Are you out of
           your tiny mind? I've just told you, I've been here
           the whole afternoon!
*JUDY comes out of the bedroom. She is wearing a very flimsy
garment.*
JUDY: What's going on, Max?
MAX looks at JUDY, then back to PETER.
MAX: Now do you believe me?

CUT TO: The Saloon Bar of The Blue Boar. Night.
*The room is now three-quarters full, and DON is busy serving
drinks. As he turns towards the cash register his expression
changes and we suddenly realise that he has caught sight of
PETER who has just entered the saloon and is crossing
towards the bar.*
PETER: Hello, Don ...
DON: Good evening, Mr Matty. I didn't expect to see
           you again this evening.
PETER: No, I don't expect you did.

DON: What would you like, sir?

PETER: I'd like a large Scotch. But I'll settle for a tomato juice.

DON: (*Relieved*) Certainly, sir.

PETER: (*Quietly*) Don, you remember the man who was sitting over there, earlier this evening – he spoke to me just as he was leaving?

DON: Yes. Mr Osborne.

PETER: Osborne – is that his name?

DON: Yes, sir.

PETER: (*Curious*) Who is he, Don?

DON: Well – I'm not really sure who he is. I believe ... he's something to do with the Arts Council.

PETER: The Arts Council?

DON: Yes, but I'm not sure.

PETER: Is he one of your regulars?

DON: No, I wouldn't say that. Although he's certainly been coming here pretty regularly during the past couple of weeks. Funny you should be interested in Mr Osborne. (*PETER looks at DON*) One lunchtime, about a week ago, you were having a drink with a friend of yours. Max Lerner, I think his name is.

PETER: Yes, that's right.

DON: Well – after you'd gone, Mr Osborne started asking me questions about him.

PETER: About Max? What sort of questions?

DON: (*Amused*) The sort you're asking me! Who is he? What does he do? Is he one of your regulars?

PETER: Were you able to satisfy his curiosity?

DON: I told him Mr Lerner was a journalist and the only thing I knew about him was that he had alimony trouble.

104

PETER:	I see. Did Mr Osborne question you about me, by any chance?
DON:	No, he didn't. It was your friend he was interested in. Would you like Worcester sauce in the tomato juice, sir?
PETER:	(*Thoughtfully*) Er – yes. Yes, I would. Thank you.

PETER sits at the bar, his thoughts obviously on DON's information about OSBORNE.

CUT TO:	The Cabin of First Edition; Poole Harbour. Evening.

PETER and CLAUDE are having coffee and are discussing the events of the past few days. PETER looks both disturbed and agitated as he listens to what his brother is saying.

CLAUDE:	It seems to me, Peter, that you've got to make your mind up. Either you want to get further involved in this business, or …
PETER:	It isn't a question of my wanting to get further involved …
CLAUDE:	(*Shaking his head*) I don't agree.
PETER:	But, Claude, just look what's happened during the past week! My flat was ransacked! I was damn nearly arrested! Max Lerner suddenly changed his mind about …
CLAUDE:	(*Stopping PETER*) Peter, listen! Please listen to me, there's a good chap! (*A moment*) I can't account for what happened during the past week. I don't know why your flat was ransacked. I don't know why Mortimer Brown switched the photographs – if he did switch them – and I haven't the slightest idea who this chap

	Osborne is. But one thing I do know! None of these things would have happened if you hadn't tried to get friendly with Phyllis Du Salle. Peter, please! Whether you like it or not you've got to make your mind up. Either you forget this girl, put her completely out of your mind, or you take the consequences. And God only knows what they might turn out to be!
PETER:	I'm sorry, Claude. I can't put her out of my mind. I've tried. It's just … no use. I've got to find her, and I've got to talk to her.
CLAUDE:	But Peter, you have talked to her! You talked to her on the telephone, and she didn't want to have anything more to do with you.
PETER:	(*Not looking at CLAUDE*) I – I don't think she was telling the truth.
CLAUDE:	That's not what you said a few minutes ago when I questioned you about the call. You said she sounded unfriendly, distinctly unfriendly, and …
PETER:	(*Irritated; angry with himself*) I know what I said a few minutes ago – and I was wrong!
CLAUDE:	Look, Peter – you asked me for my opinion and I'm giving it to you! If you continue with this affair, if you insist on … (*He stops*)

CLAUDE has obviously heard something; so has PETER.

MRS FRINTON: (*Off; calling*) Mr Matty – it's Mrs Frinton!

After a moment, MRS FRINTON appears.

MRS FRINTON:	(*To PETER*) Sorry to disturb you, but there's been a phone message for you from a Mrs Cassidy.
PETER:	(*Surprised*) Mrs Cassidy?
MRS FRINTON:	Yes, dearie.
CLAUDE:	(*To PETER*) Who's Mrs Cassidy? I seem to know the name.
PETER:	She's Sir Arnold Wyatt's housekeeper. (*Curious*) What did she say, Mrs Frinton?
MRS FRINTON:	She said she'd like you to meet her tomorrow morning, if possible. She'll be in Fletcher's Café about eleven o'clock.
PETER:	Fletcher's Café – that's in Heatherdown.
MRS FRINTON:	That's right.
PETER:	Is that all she said?
MRS FRINTON:	No, she said she wanted to explain about the photograph.
CLAUDE:	The photograph?
MRS FRINTON:	That's what she said, dearie.

A slight pause.

PETER:	(*Quietly*) Thank you, Mrs Frinton. Oh – would you like a cup of coffee, or a drink perhaps?
MRS FRINTON:	No, thank you. That's very kind of you, but I must get back. I'm trying to do my accounts and – oh, dear! – I'm in a frightful muddle, I'm afraid.

MRS FRINTON smiles at CLAUDE and goes out. After a brief glance at his brother, PETER follows her.

CUT TO: A road in Heatherdown. Morning.
PETER has parked his Jaguar on a meter and is getting out of the car, about to make his way towards Fletcher's Café. He

locks the car and then strolls thoughtfully towards the turning at the end of the road leading into the main street.

CUT TO: The Main Street of Heatherdown. Morning.

PETER turns the corner and walks, deep in thought, in the direction of Fletcher's Café and MORTIMER BROWN's shop. After a while he looks up and his steps gradually slow down as he stares in obvious surprise at something ahead of him.

We suddenly see what he is looking at. Three police cars and an ambulance are drawn up outside of MORTIMER BROWN's shop. One of the police cars is parked away from the kerb and its blue light is flashing. Two plain-clothes men – SERGEANT ROY COLFORD and INSPECTOR TOM LANE – are standing in front of the window in earnest conversation.

A fair-sized crowd of onlookers has gathered; others are crossing the road to join them. Two Constables are advising the onlookers to keep away from the area around the doorway of the shop.

As PETER hurries towards the scene and joins the onlookers, ambulance men emerge from the shop carrying a stretcher. The body on the stretcher is completely covered by a blanket. PETER elbows his way through the crowd, finally stopping to watch the ambulance men load the stretcher into the ambulance. After a moment, and obviously curious, he turns towards a couple of onlookers.

PETER: What's happened, d'you know?

1st MAN: There's been a murder …

PETER: Murder?

2nd MAN: (*To PETER*) It's the chap who owns the place …

1st MAN: The photographer.

PETER: (*Staggered*) Mortimer Brown?

1st MAN: That's right.

PETER: He's been murdered?

2nd MAN: (*Nodding*) I think so.

PETER stares at the man for a moment, then as he turns away, he notices that one of the plain-clothes men – DETECTIVE SERGEANT COLFORD – is saying goodbye to his colleagues. As COLFORD crosses towards one of the police cars, PETER makes a decision to join him. COLFORD looks up as PETER approaches.

PETER: Excuse me, Officer. What happened?

COLFORD looks at PETER for a second or two, weighing him up, before replying.

COLFORD: There's been a murder, sir.

PETER: Yes, I know. But what happened, exactly? How was he murdered?

COLFORD: (*Puzzled*) He?

PETER: Mr Brown.

A slight pause.

COLFORD points to the door of the photographer's shop and PETER looks in the direction he is pointing. A worried looking MORTIMER BROWN has emerged from the shop and is now standing in the doorway talking to INSPECTOR LANE. After a moment, PETER slowly turns towards COLFORD again.

PETER: Then who was murdered?

COLFORD: A woman, sir. A Mrs Cassidy.

END OF EPISODE TWO

EPISODE THREE

OPEN TO: The Main Street in Heatherdown. Morning.

PETER is staring at COLFORD in amazement. In the background we can see MORTIMER BROWN in earnest conversation with INSPECTOR LANE.

PETER: What happened to Mrs Cassidy?

COLFORD: I've told you. She was murdered.

PETER: (*Tensely*) Yes, I know. But how was she murdered? What happened, exactly?

COLFORD: Are you a reporter?

PETER: No. But … (*He hesitates, then:*) I knew Mrs Cassidy, slightly. I had an appointment with her.

COLFORD: (*Immediately interested in this information*) When – this morning?

PETER: Yes, at eleven o'clock.

COLFORD: Tell me about this appointment, sir.

PETER: I was supposed to meet her in the café, the one across the road. She telephoned a friend of mine last night and … (*He stops*) You still haven't answered my question. How was she murdered?

COLFORD: (*After a moment*) She was shot. She'd just entered the photographer's when, according to Mr Brown, a car raced by and someone fired several shots. Mrs Cassidy was hit.

PETER: When did this happen?

COLFORD: About twenty minutes ago.

PETER: Were the shots intended for Mrs Cassidy?

COLFORD: That's a good question, sir. We're not sure.

Both PETER and COLFORD now turn towards the INSPECTOR who, having concluded his conversation with BROWN, is about to join them.

COLFORD: (*To the INSPECTOR*) This gentleman had an appointment with Mrs Cassidy.

LANE: (*Looking at PETER*) Indeed?

COLFORD: They were supposed to meet in Fletcher's.

LANE: Was Mrs Cassidy a friend of yours, sir?

PETER: No. She ... worked for Sir Arnold Wyatt. She was his housekeeper.

LANE: Yes, we know that. But was she a friend of yours?

PETER: No, she wasn't, but she telephoned me last night and said that she wanted to see me ... (*Hesitatingly*) My name is Matty. Peter Matty. I'm a publisher. I live in London, but I've got a boat down here ... or rather ... in Poole Harbour. Several weeks ago, I had occasion to visit Sir Arnold Wyatt and Mrs Cassidy happened to be ... (*With a glance at the onlookers*) Look, I'm sorry, this is impossible! We can't talk here ...

LANE: I agree, Mr Matty. Let's go down to the station. Have you a car?

PETER: Yes.

LANE: Then perhaps you'd get your car and follow us, sir.

PETER: Er – yes, all right.

PETER hesitates, then with a little nod turns and walks away. COLFORD and the INSPECTOR watch him as he disappears into the crowd.

COLFORD: Peter Matty. Have you heard of him?

LANE: (*Thoughtfully*) I'm not sure. I seem to know the name.

CUT TO: The Entrance to HEATHERDOWN Railway Station. Afternoon.

A train has just arrived from London and passengers are emerging from the narrow lane leading down to the platform.

114

SIR ARNOLD WYATT is amongst the passengers. He is carrying a brief case and looks to be deep in thought as he crosses to one of the waiting taxis. The driver of the car switches off his radio, jumps out of the driving seat, and opens the passenger door. WYATT gets into the car.

CUT TO: The Drive of Forest Gate Manor, Heatherdown. Afternoon.

A police car is on the drive and INSPECTOR LANE accompanied by the uniformed driver, is standing on the drive peering in one of the windows. Somewhere in the background a bell is ringing. After a little while the bell stops and SERGEANT COLFORD emerges from the porch of the house.

COLFORD: There's no one in. The place appears to be deserted.

LANE: All right. We'll come back later.

The driver gets into the car and is about to be followed by LANE when COLFORD suddenly puts a restraining hand on the INSPECTOR's shoulder. He nods towards the main gate. The taxi has entered the drive and is approaching the house. Immediately the taxi stops, SIR ARNOLD jumps out. He looks at the police car with obvious curiosity.

LANE: (*Approaching*) Sir Arnold Wyatt?

WYATT: Yes?

LANE: I'm Detective Inspector Lane, sir.

WYATT: Yes, I know. I recognised you, Inspector. What is it? Has something happened? (*He looks at the house*) Don't tell me my house has been broken into?

LANE: No, sir. It's your housekeeper – Mrs Cassidy. I'm afraid … she's dead, sir.

WYATT: (*Stunned*) Good God!

CUT TO: SIR ARNOLD WYATT's Study. Afternoon.

WYATT is sitting on the settee, a glass of whisky in his hand. He looks very distressed as he listens to the INSPECTOR and SERGEANT COLFORD.

LANE: … I know exactly how you feel, sir, and believe me I have no wish to make a nuisance of myself, but I'd be very grateful if you could answer one or two questions.

WYATT: Yes. Yes, of course. I'm sorry, Inspector. It was such a shock. But tell me, please … What happened? You say she was shot?

LANE: Yes. Mrs Cassidy had just entered the shop – Mortimer Brown's. A shot was fired – presumably from the street, but we're not sure – and Mrs Cassidy was hit. She died almost immediately.

WYATT: But why on earth should anyone want to kill my housekeeper? It's just doesn't make sense!

LANE: When did you last see Mrs Cassidy, sir?

WYATT: This morning. I left the house about eight o'clock. I took my little granddaughter up to London. She's staying the weekend with some friends of mine.

LANE: You caught the eight-forty-five?

WYATT: Yes, that's right. Well – in theory the eight-forty-five. It was nearly ten past nine when we left Heatherdown.

LANE: And you left Mrs Cassidy here, in the house?

WYATT nods.

LANE: Was she alone?

WYATT: Yes.

LANE: Did Mrs Cassidy tell you that she would be going into the village later in the morning?

WYATT: Yes, I think she said she was going to do some shopping.

LANE: Did she mention that she would be calling at Mortimer Brown's?

WYATT: No, she didn't.

LANE: Why did she call on Mr Brown, sir – have you any idea?

WYATT: No, I'm afraid I haven't. I should ask Mr Brown.

LANE: We have done, sir. He doesn't know why she wanted to see him.

WYATT: Neither do I, Inspector.

LANE: (*After a tiny hesitation*) Just one more question, sir, then we'll leave you in peace. Did you know that Mrs Cassidy had an appointment this morning with a man called Peter Matty?

WYATT: (*Surprised*) No, I didn't.

LANE: You know Mr Matty, sir?

WYATT: Yes, I do. He's a publisher. He called round to see me about … But what makes you think Mrs Cassidy had an appointment with him?

LANE: According to Mr Matty, your housekeeper telephoned him last night and asked to see him. They arranged to meet this morning in Heatherdown.

WYATT: Well – this is news to me, Inspector! I certainly knew nothing about the appointment.

LANE: (*With a little nod, closing the interview*) Thank you, sir.

CUT TO: Inside PETER's Car. Night.

PETER is driving his car on the outskirts of Heatherdown heading towards Forest Gate Manor. CLAUDE is in the passenger seat. There is a parcel on his lap; his most recent LP.

PETER: I appreciate what you're doing, Claude.

117

CLAUDE: (*Not unfriendly*) So you should, because I'm dead against it.

PETER: Claude, it's no use, I've got to find out what the hell this is all about! I've got to find out why Mrs Cassidy wanted to talk to me!

CLAUDE: Well, you know my views on all this. I don't have to reiterate them.

PETER: You think I should call it a day and forget what happened this morning?

CLAUDE: (*Hesitating*) Yes, I do.

PETER: You don't sound very convincing.

CLAUDE: Peter, I understand how you feel and if I were in your shoes, I should probably feel the same. (*Shaking his head*) But I'm worried. I really don't like it.

PETER: What is it you don't like?

CLAUDE: I don't like the fact that your flat was ransacked, and I don't like the fact that shortly after she contacted you Mrs Cassidy was murdered.

PETER: In other words, you think something unpleasant could very easily happen to me?

CLAUDE: If you continue to become involved in this affair – yes, I do.

PETER: Yes, well – if you don't want to go ahead with this, just say so. There'll be no hard feelings, I assure you.

CLAUDE: No, no, I'll go ahead with it.

PETER: Sir Arnold's far more likely to confide in you, Claude. I'm sure of that.

CLAUDE: If he has anything to confide. (*A pause*) You want me to try and find out whether he knew about your appointment with Mrs Cassidy?

PETER: And if he did know, then what was it all about?

CLAUDE: (*Nodding*) Well – we'll see what we can do.

CUT TO: The Study of Forest Gate Manor. Night.

SIR ARNOLD is sitting in an armchair listening to music from his record player and restlessly glancing at the pages of an art book. He looks tired and depressed. The doorbell rings and after consulting his watch – he is obviously expecting a visitor – he puts the book down, turns off the record player, and goes out into the hall.

CUT TO: The Hall of Forest Gate Manor. Night.

WYATT enters the hall and opens the front door. CLAUDE is standing in the porch, parcel in hand. WYATT stares at him in obvious surprise. CLAUDE is certainly not the person he expected.

CLAUDE: Good evening, Sir Arnold.

WYATT: Why – hello, Mr Matty!

CLAUDE: I hope I'm not disturbing you.

WYATT: (*A shade embarrassed*) No. No, not at all.

CLAUDE: Could you spare me a few minutes?

WYATT: Yes, of course! Please come in!

CLAUDE enters the hall.

CLAUDE: (*As WYATT closes the front door*) Thank you.

WYATT: Do forgive me, I was expecting someone else, and I didn't immediately recognise you.

CLAUDE: (*Offering the parcel*) I thought you might like this. It's a new recording of mine, the one I mentioned. I received copies this morning.

WYATT: (*Taking the LP*) How very thoughtful of you! This really is most kind. Come into the study, Mr Matty!

CUT TO: The Study of Forest Gate Manor. Night.

CLAUDE enters followed by WYATT who, after closing the door behind him, puts the LP down on the arm of the sofa.

WYATT: Can I offer you a drink?

119

CLAUDE: No, I don't think so, thank you.

WYATT: It's curious you should call. I intended to get in touch with you, or rather your brother, first thing tomorrow morning.

CLAUDE: About Mrs Cassidy?

WYATT: (*Softly*) Yes.

CLAUDE: My brother was in Heatherdown this morning shortly after she was shot.

WYATT: Yes – the police told me.

CLAUDE: It must have been a terrible shock to you. When I heard the news, I was appalled, I couldn't believe it …

WYATT: (*Distressed*) Yes, I know. I know … Even now I just can't believe it's happened. I was in London. I knew nothing about it, absolutely nothing, until I arrived home.

CLAUDE: Have the police any idea who did it?

WYATT: I don't think so. If they have, they certainly haven't confided in me. It's utterly and completely beyond my comprehension why anyone should want to kill my housekeeper. But please, do sit down!

CLAUDE looks around the room, finally sitting in the chair previously occupied by SIR ARNOLD.

WYATT: Are you sure I can't offer you a drink?

CLAUDE: Yes, I'm sure, thank you.

WYATT crosses to the table and carries the art book over to his desk.

WYATT: How's your brother, Mr Matty? He's well, I trust?

CLAUDE: Yes, he is, but I'm afraid he's very bewildered at the moment, and very upset. He had an appointment to see Mrs Cassidy. That's why he was in Heatherdown.

WYATT moves to the sofa and sits facing CLAUDE.

WYATT: (*Quietly*) Yes, I know.

CLAUDE: You knew about the appointment?

WYATT: The Inspector told me about it, and I must confess I was very surprised. I didn't realise that your brother and Mrs Cassidy were acquainted.

CLAUDE: I don't think they were.

WYATT: Then who made the appointment?

CLAUDE: Mrs Cassidy did. She telephoned Peter, or rather she left a message for him, asking him to meet her in Fletcher's café.

WYATT: (*Puzzled*) Now why on earth should she do that?

CLAUDE: She said she wanted to explain about the photograph. I can only assume that she meant the photograph of your daughter, the one that was in Brown's window. The one my brother mistook for Phyllis Du Salle.

WYATT: I find this very odd. Was this the first time Mrs Cassidy had contacted your brother?

CLAUDE: As far as I know. Sir Arnold, forgive my asking, but did you discuss my brother with your housekeeper? Did you tell her what happened the morning we went to Mortimer Brown's?

WYATT: (*A moment, then:*) Yes, I did.

CLAUDE: And what was her reaction?

WYATT: She thought your brother was imagining things. She thought he'd become so obsessed by this Mrs Du Salle that he was … well …

CLAUDE: Unbalanced?

WYATT: Yes.

CLAUDE: Is that what *you* think?

121

WYATT:	(*Obviously perplexed*) I just don't know what to think. I'm so bewildered by the turn of events and by what happened to Mrs Cassidy that … (*He stops; looks at CLAUDE for a moment, hesitates, then makes a decision*) Mr Matty, I shouldn't tell you this. I promised not to. I promised not to say a word to anyone, but … (*Shaking his head*) … it's no use, I've just got to confide in you. (*After a tiny pause*) Twenty-four hours before I first met your brother, a man called Osborne telephoned me. He said he wanted to see me, urgently. When I asked him what it was he wanted to see me about he said: "I want to talk to you about a very old friend of yours, Sir Arnold – Norman Du Salle."
CLAUDE:	Norman Du Salle? (*Puzzled*) Was Du Salle a friend of yours?
WYATT:	(*Quietly*) Yes, he was.
CLAUDE:	(*Angrily*) But that's not what you told Peter! You told Peter you'd never heard of him …
WYATT:	(*Stopping CLAUDE*) Yes – yes, I know what I told your brother, Mr Matty! But – please listen to me! Listen to what I've got to say …

CUT TO: The Drive of Forest Gate Manor. Night.
A Rover 2000 enters the drive and stops in front of the house. JULIAN OSBORNE gets out of the car and after taking a briefcase from the back seat crosses towards the porch.

CUT TO: The Porch of Forest Gate Manor. Night.
Osborne is ringing the front doorbell. We hear the bell ringing inside the house. After a moment he presses the button

again. Pause. He rings the bell for the third time and as he does so the door suddenly opens.

WYATT: Sorry to have kept you waiting.

OSBORNE: Good evening, Sir Arnold. I'm a little late. I think I said eight o'clock.

WYATT: Yes, I … was expecting you earlier. Come in.

OSBORNE looks at WYATT, struck by his manner, then with a nod enters the hall.

CUT TO: The Hall of Forest Gate Manor. Night.

WYATT: Let me take your coat.

OSBORNE: Thank you.

As OSBORNE takes off his things, he quietly watches WYATT, aware of the fact that SIR ARNOLD is avoiding looking at him as he places the coat and scarf in a nearby cupboard.

OSBORNE: Are you alone?

WYATT: No. I was just going to tell you. I've … got a visitor, I'm afraid.

OSBORNE: That's all right. I can wait.

WYATT: It's Mr Matty.

OSBORNE: (*Surprised*) Peter Matty?

WYATT: No, it's his brother – Claude.

OSBORNE: You never told me Claude Matty was a friend of yours?

WYATT: You never asked me. In any case, he's not a friend of mine.

OSBORNE: Then what's he doing here?

WYATT: Ostensibly he brought me a present, a gramophone record. But I'm afraid it was painfully obvious the record was just an excuse. He wanted to talk about his brother and … what happened to Mrs Cassidy.

OSBORNE: (*A moment; then:*) Well – in that case perhaps you'd better introduce me, and we'll

123

put him in the picture. (*With the flicker of a smile*) That is, of course, if you haven't already done so.

WYATT stares at OSBORNE, surprised by this remark; then obviously somewhat relieved he turns and opens the study door.

CUT TO: A road near Forest Gate Manor. Night.
PETER's car is parked in this quiet road near SIR ARNOLD WYATT's house. PETER is sitting at the wheel, smoking a cigarette and anxiously awaiting the return of his brother. The car radio is playing.

CUT TO: Inside PETER's Car. Night.
PETER looks at his watch, hesitates, then after switching off the radio he stubs out his cigarette in the ashtray. He is in the process of doing this when he notices – through the windscreen – that someone is approaching. As the figure draws near, he recognises CLAUDE and jumps out of the car.

CUT TO: A road near Forest Gate Manor. Night.
CLAUDE arrives at the Jaguar.
PETER: You've been a devil of a time …
CLAUDE: Yes, I know.
PETER: I was getting quite worried. Did you see Wyatt?
CLAUDE's expression is serious.
CLAUDE: Yes, I did. Not only Wyatt. Peter, let's get in the car.
PETER: (*Taking hold of CLAUDE's arm*) What do you mean – not only Wyatt? Who else did you see?
CLAUDE: I saw the man you told me about. The man in the pub – the one who spoke to you.

124

PETER:	Osborne?
CLAUDE:	That's right. Julian Osborne. He arrived shortly after I did.
PETER:	(*Puzzled*) Osborne did?
CLAUDE:	Yes.
PETER:	Is he a friend of Wyatt's?
CLAUDE:	No – not exactly.
PETER:	Then what was he doing there?
CLAUDE:	(*Quietly*) Let's get in the car.
PETER:	Claude, who is this man?
CLAUDE:	He's with Scotland Yard; attached to the Special Branch.
PETER:	(*Softly*) Good God!
CLAUDE:	Get in the car, Peter. We're going back to the house. (*PETER looks at CLAUDE*) Osborne wants to talk to you.

CUT TO: SIR ARNOLD WYATT's Study. Night.
Although Sir Arnold is at the drinks table quietly mixing himself a whisky and soda, one senses a tense atmosphere in the room. CLAUDE and JULIAN OSBORNE have drinks but PETER has refused one. He is standing near the sofa looking down at OSBORNE, a look of irritation on his face.

PETER:	(*To OSBORNE*) All right – I accept who you are, and what you are! Now get to the point.
OSBORNE:	Which particular point have you got in mind, sir?
PETER:	My brother said you wanted to talk to me.
OSBORNE:	Yes, I thought perhaps, under the circumstances, that might be a good idea. (*Rising*) But I'm beginning to wonder. (*He faces PETER; a note of authority in his voice*) Mr Matty, I realise that you've been extremely worried just recently, and I must

admit, to a certain extent I've been responsible. But believe me, no one's been trying to make a fool out of you, as you seem to be suggesting. Now be sensible, just relax and listen to what Sir Arnold and I have to tell you.

PETER hesitates, looks at CLAUDE, then with a little nod crosses down to one of the armchairs.

WYATT: (*Moving down to Peter and offering him the whisky*) Are you sure you won't have a drink?

PETER: (*Shaking his head; but not unfriendly*) Thank you – no.

WYATT turns and sits on the arm of the settee.

WYATT: Many years ago, I befriended a young man called Norman Du Salle. He was the son of a very dear friend of mine. Norman was an ambitious boy and immediately he was twenty-one he emigrated to America. He made a success over there and for several years wrote a newspaper column which was widely syndicated. Then about seven or eight years ago his work deteriorated somewhat, and his column was discontinued. During the course of his career, however, as you can well imagine, he met a great many important people. Presidents, Prime Ministers, Ambassadors, famous actors, business tycoons – he met them all. And invariably he gathered information about them. Confidential information, about their private affairs. I regret to say, in recent years, he made use of that information.

PETER: You mean – blackmail?

WYATT: Yes, Mr Matty. Blackmail. (*A pause*) About
                seven years ago, a young man named Martin
                Clifford called on me. He was an American, a
                freelance journalist, and he had a letter of
                introduction from Norman – whom,
                incidentally, I hadn't seen since he emigrated.
                Martin was a strange young man, but since he
                was a friend of Norman's I invited him to stay
                with me. He stayed for several weeks and
                eventually, I regret to say … married my
                daughter.

OSBORNE: (*Quietly*) Go on, Sir Arnold.

WYATT: Although I never liked Martin it was only
                recently, quite recently, in fact, that I learned
                the truth about him from Mr Osborne. I'm
                ashamed to say it … he worked for Norman.

PETER: I see.

OSBORNE: Unfortunately, Du Salle's activities were not
                confined to the United States. He had an
                important contact in this country – a man
                called George Delta. When Mrs Du Salle
                decided to visit England, we felt sure that
                sooner or later Delta would try and get in
                touch with her. And that, for the record, is
                when we became interested in you, Mr Matty.

PETER: In me?

OSBORNE: Yes.

PETER: But … why me?

OSBORNE: You spoke to Mrs Du Salle on the plane. You
                made a point of getting friendly with her.
                You tried to take her out to dinner. In short …
                we thought you were George Delta!

CUT TO: The entrance to Poole Harbour. Morning.
A large car, driven by a uniformed driver, arrives at the entrance to the harbour. OSBORNE and PHYLLIS DU SALLE are sitting in the back of the car. The car slows down as it approaches the quay.

CUT TO: Inside the Car.
OSBORNE is staring at PHYLLIS who, somewhat nervously, is looking out of the window at the marina. She suddenly realises that she is being stared at and quickly turns her head. OSBORNE gives her a reassuring smile.

PHYLLIS: You're sure he's expecting me?
OSBORNE: You've asked me that question before …
PHYLLIS: Yes, I know …
OSBORNE: I'm quite sure. I imagine he'll take you out to lunch. We'll pick you up at three o'clock.
PHYLLIS: Supposing he doesn't?
OSBORNE: (*Smiling*) Then we'll both be disappointed.

CUT TO: Poole Harbour. Morning.
The car draws to a standstill about twenty or thirty yards short of where PETER's boat First Edition is moored. PHYLLIS gets out of the car and turns to speak to OSBORNE who is winding down his window. PETER emerges from the cabin on the boat. OSBORNE suddenly sees him and nods towards the boat. PHYLLIS quickly turns. For a little while PETER and PHYLLIS stare at each other, then PETER's face breaks into a smile and he gives a friendly wave.

CUT TO: The Cabin of First Edition. Morning.
PETER and PHYLLIS are having a drink before going out to lunch. There is a bottle of sherry on the table, together with a packet of cigarettes and a lighter.

PHYLLIS: ... Believe me, Peter, I never for one moment thought that you were involved. I told Osborne so, the very first time we met, but he just wouldn't believe me. He must have asked me a hundred times what we talked about the day you brought me down here.

PETER: He thought I worked for your husband ...

PHYLLIS: Yes, I know ...

PETER: ... That I was the man they'd been looking for – George Delta.

PHYLLIS: Yes, he told me.

PETER: Had you heard of Delta before Osborne mentioned him?

PHYLLIS: Yes. Linda Braithwaite mentioned his name. We were having a drink together one evening, in Geneva, and suddenly, quite out of the blue, she asked me if I knew him.

PETER: Did you tell Osborne that?

PHYLLIS: I didn't have to tell him.

PETER: What do you mean?

PHYLLIS: Linda worked for Osborne. That's why she got friendly with me in Switzerland. Why she followed me to London. I had certain letters and tape recordings which belonged to Norman and they thought ... They were frightened I was going to hand them over to you – or rather, George Delta.

PETER: I see. (*A moment*) You know what happened to Mrs Braithwaite?

PHYLLIS: Yes, I know. I was actually staying with her the day she was murdered. She'd been to a meeting at Scotland Yard and was on her way home when George Delta picked her up – at least, that's the theory.

PETER: You say you were staying with her?

PHYLLIS: Yes. It was Osborne's idea that I went into hiding. He was worried about my safety. He said until they'd identified Delta, my life was in danger. He was very persuasive, Peter. I really had no alternative.

PETER: When did you first meet Osborne?

PHYLLIS: The day you brought me down here; the day I borrowed your car. You remember I'd spoken to Sir Arnold on the phone, and he'd invited me to spend the weekend with him …

CUT TO: The Drive of Forest Gate Manor. Afternoon.

PETER's Jaguar, driven by PHYLLIS, enters the drive of Forest Gate Manor and proceeds towards the house. A police car is parked on the drive, near the porch, and a young officer by the name of BOB KESWICK is sitting at the wheel, glancing through the pages of a magazine. He looks up as he hears the approaching car. Through the windscreen of the police car, we see the Jaguar slowly come to a standstill.

PHYLLIS stares at the police car with obvious curiosity as she gets out of the Jaguar and takes her case from the back seat. KESWICK puts down the magazine and gets out of the police car. He gives PHYLLIS a friendly little salute as he approaches her.

KESWICK: Mrs Du Salle?

PHYLLIS: (*Puzzled*) Yes?

KESWICK: Let me take your case, madam.

PHYLLIS hesitates.

PHYLLIS: Er – thank you …

KESWICK takes the case, enters the porch, and rings the doorbell. PHYLLIS stands by his side, obviously a shade bewildered.

Pause.

KESWICK: It's a lovely day.
PHYLLIS: Yes, it is …
KESWICK: Have you driven far?
PHYLLIS: No, just from … Not very far.
The door is opened by MRS CASSIDY.
KESWICK: Would you tell Sir Arnold that Mrs Du
                 Salle has arrived?
MRS CASSIDY: Yes, certainly. (*To PHYLLIS*) Please come
                 in …
*MRS CASSIDY reaches out for the case, but KESWICK
quickly shakes his head.*
KESWICK: (*Pleasantly; not at all officious*) It's quite
                 all right. I'll take care of this. (*To
                 PHYLLIS*) You go ahead, madam.
*Still bewildered, PHYLLIS enters the house, turning to look
back at KESWICK as she does so. She is surprised to see that
he is on his way back to the police car with her suitcase.*

CUT TO: The Hall of Forest Gate Manor. Afternoon.
*MRS CASSIDY leads PHYLLIS towards the study door. She
knocks on the door, then opening it, beckons PHYLLIS to
enter.*

CUT TO: SIR ARNOLD WYATT's Study. Afternoon.
*PHYLLIS slowly enters the study, then stops dead, staring at
the occupants of the room in amazement. LINDA
BRAITHWAITE is at the far end of the room talking to a
distinguished looking man in police uniform. She quickly
turns towards the door as PHYLLIS appears. JULIAN
OSBORNE is standing near the fireplace in earnest
conversation with SIR ARNOLD. Their conversation ceases
the moment PHYLLIS enters. For a brief moment the two men
stare at PHYLLIS, seemingly weighing her up, then SIR
ARNOLD moves slowly down to her and holds out his hand.*

131

WYATT: Mrs Du Salle?

PHYLLIS: … Yes.

WYATT: I'm Sir Arnold Wyatt. May I introduce you to Chief-Superintendent Galloway and Mr Julian Osborne. Mrs Braithwaite I think you've already met.

CUT TO: The Cabin of First Edition. Morning.

PHYLLIS: … I was so amazed at seeing Linda Braithwaite that it must have been at least two or three minutes before I realised that Osborne was talking to me – talking about my husband. And then gradually it dawned on me that at long last, Peter, I was learning the truth about Norman. It has to be the truth because … it explained so many things.

PETER: What sort of things, Phyllis?

PHYLLIS: When Norman lost his job, he was worried, deeply worried about money. And then suddenly the whole situation changed. He literally had money to burn. When I questioned him about this, he told me he'd been asked to write a series of articles for a German newspaper and that they'd paid him an enormous sum of money in advance … (*She stops*)

CLAUDE has entered the cabin; he carries a number of parcels and has obviously been shopping. He stares at PHYLLIS in obvious surprise. PETER smilingly rises from the table.

PETER: Phyllis, I want you to meet my brother. Claude, this is Mrs Du … Phyllis.

PHYLLIS: I'm delighted to meet you. I enjoyed your concert in Geneva enormously.

CLAUDE: Thank you. That's very kind of you.

132

CLAUDE puts down his parcels and shakes hands with PHYLLIS. There is a faintly embarrassed pause.

PETER: What have you been doing, buying up the village?

CLAUDE: Very nearly.

PETER: We're just about to drive into Bournemouth for lunch – why not join us?

CLAUDE: Er – no, thanks a lot, but I've one or two things I'd like to see to.

PHYLLIS: Please – we'd love you to come …

CLAUDE: No, really, it's very nice of you both, but … I've got several letters I must write, and I had an enormous breakfast this morning. (*Patting his stomach*) I swore I'd skip lunch today.

PETER: (*To PHYLLIS*) This is nonsense! He's a half-a-grapefruit man! He's just being tactful! All right, Claude! (*Taking hold of PHYLLIS's arm*) We'll see you later.

PHYLLIS smiles at CLAUDE as she rises from the table and goes out with PETER. CLAUDE moves down to the table and stands thoughtfully staring down at the empty glasses and the bottle of sherry. It is difficult to tell what he is thinking.

A pause.

PETER suddenly returns.

PETER: Forgot my wallet!

PETER crosses to a side drawer and takes out his wallet and some loose change. As he turns, he hesitates for a moment, looking across at CLAUDE.

PETER: Well – what do you think of her?

CLAUDE: (*His thoughts elsewhere*) What?

PETER: I said: what do you think of her?

CLAUDE: Oh – she's … better looking than I expected.

PETER grins and goes out.

CUT TO: A Road near Bournemouth.
PHYLLIS is driving PETER's car again and they are on the outskirts of Bournemouth. It is fairly obvious that PETER is enjoying the journey.

CUT TO: Inside PETER's car. Day.
PETER: You still haven't told me where you're staying.
PHYLLIS: At the moment I'm staying at a small hotel near – just outside London.
PETER: Was that Osborne's idea?
PHYLLIS: Yes. He made me go into hiding. He was frightened that you, or rather George Delta, might contact me. Apparently, Delta's under the impression I have information which could be of value to him.
PETER: Information you got from your husband?
PHYLLIS: Yes.
PETER: And have you?
PHYLLIS: No, I haven't. (*A moment*) Peter, I'm sorry I can't tell you the name of my hotel, but I promised Osborne I wouldn't tell anyone where I was staying, not even you, and I don't want him to think …
PETER: That's all right, I understand! I understand perfectly – but how am I going to get in touch with you again?
PHYLLIS: When are you going back to London?
PETER: Probably the day after tomorrow.
PHYLLIS: I'll phone your office first thing on Monday morning.
PETER: Is that a promise?
PHYLLIS smiles at PETER and nods.

134

CUT TO: The Cabin of First Edition. Day.

CLAUDE is sitting at the table studying a sheet of music and eating the remains of a bar of chocolate. Voices are heard, followed by the sound of a departing car. CLAUDE rises and puts the manuscript in a weekend case which is on a nearby chair. As he closes the case and locks it PETER enters the cabin. He is smoking a cigar and looks distinctly pleased with life.

CLAUDE: Hello, Peter! If appearances are anything to go by, the lunch was a success!

PETER: Very much so. You should have joined us.

CLAUDE: And made an enemy for life?

PETER laughs and sits at the table.

PETER: Didn't you have anything to eat?

CLAUDE: I made myself a sandwich and bought a bar of chocolate. That's all I wanted. (*He joins PETER at the table*) When are you seeing Phyllis again?

PETER: Next week. She's promised to phone me on Monday morning. (*He notices the case*) Why the case?

CLAUDE: Oh – I was just going to tell you. It's a damn nuisance but I've got to go up to Scotland. I shall be back on Monday or Tuesday.

PETER: Are you giving a recital?

CLAUDE: No, as a matter of fact I'm trying to get out of giving one. But they won't take "No" for an answer.

PETER: When are you leaving?

CLAUDE: This afternoon.

PETER: (*Surprised*) This afternoon?

CLAUDE: I plan to catch the 3.15. Perhaps you'd run me to the station?

PETER: Yes, of course. Are you flying up?

CLAUDE:	No, I've managed to get a sleeper. My agent's meeting me at Euston. But tell me about your lunch. What happened?
PETER:	I thought I'd had a pretty tough time during the past few weeks, but believe me, it's nothing compared with what Phyllis has been through.
CLAUDE:	I can believe that.
PETER:	There seems to be little doubt that Norman Du Salle has incriminating information about certain people in this country. Important people. Scotland Yard were under the impression Phyllis also had this information and they were frightened she might be abducted.
CLAUDE:	By George Delta?
PETER:	Yes.
CLAUDE:	I see. (*A pause, then:*) Did Phyllis explain about Harley Street, and what happened in the taxi?
PETER:	Yes. For some time, Osborne laboured under the delusion that I was Delta. Phyllis wasn't convinced of this, so in the end they agreed to test me out. The scene in Harley Street was closely watched by the Special Branch and, fortunately for me, my behaviour convinced them that my interest in Phyllis was, well, purely of a personal nature. Later, at Osborne's request, she telephoned me and – not to put too fine a point on it – gave me the brush off.

CLAUDE:	But after Phyllis telephoned you, if I remember rightly ... (*He stops, having heard a noise on deck*)
MRS FRINTON:	(*Off*) Anybody at home?
PETER:	(*Rising*) It's Mrs Frinton.

MRS FRINTON appears down the gangway. She carries a parcel of books and several letters.

MRS FRINTON:	Sorry to disturb you, Mr Matty, but these books arrived by the second post. I thought they might be important.

PETER takes the parcel and the letters.

PETER:	Thank you, Mrs Frinton. That's very kind of you.

MRS FRINTON gives a friendly nod, then turns her attention to CLAUDE.

MRS FRINTON:	And your phone call was one-seventy, sir. I checked with the operator.
CLAUDE:	(*Faintly embarrassed*) Oh – thank you, Mrs Frinton.

CLAUDE takes out his wallet, extracts a pound note, sorts out the various change in his pocket, and finally hands MRS FRINTON the money. He is aware of the fact that PETER is watching him.

CLAUDE:	One-seventy ...
MRS FRINTON:	Thank you, sir.
CLAUDE:	(*Recovering his composure*) Thank <u>you</u>, Mrs Frinton.

MRS FRINTON smiles at PETER and goes.

PETER:	One pound seventy ... That must have been quite a phone call.
CLAUDE:	Yes. It was to Scotland. I was talking for ages.
PETER:	(*Looking at CLAUDE; curious*) You must have been.

137

CUT TO: The Continental Departures Building, Heathrow. Evening.

A taxi pulls up outside the building and MORTIMER BROWN gets out. After hurriedly paying the driver, he lifts his suitcase out of the cab, shakes his head somewhat impatiently at an approaching porter, and hurries into the building.

CUT TO: A British Airways Desk. Heathrow.

Two UNIFORMED GIRLS are checking tickets and sorting through various documents when CLAUDE approaches the desk. His manner is serious, a shade tense. One of the girls looks up and immediately recognises him.

GIRL: Mr Matty?

CLAUDE: Yes.

GIRL: Your ticket's ready for you, sir.

CLAUDE: Thank you.

The GIRL opens a drawer and takes out a first-class air ticket.

GIRL: Flight BE 034. First class to Rome. Checking-in time 1820. I think you asked for an open return, sir?

CLAUDE: Yes, that's right.

GIRL: Have you got your passport?

CLAUDE: Yes, I have. May I pay by cheque?

GIRL: Yes, of course, Mr Matty.

The GIRL examines the ticket as CLAUDE produces his cheque book and takes out his pen.

CUT TO: MOLLIE STAFFORD's Office. Morning.

A faintly disgruntled MOLLIE is busy typing a contract when PETER enters carrying several books and a number of letters.

PETER: Good morning, Mollie.

MOLLIE: Morning.

PETER: (*Taking off his things*) I've been stuck in a traffic block for twenty-five minutes, I thought I was never going to get here!

MOLLIE: You should try walking. There's a pile of letters on your desk and there's been at least half-a-dozen phone calls.

PETER: I don't suppose a Mrs Du Salle has telephoned?

MOLLIE: Yes, she has. You've just missed her – about two minutes ago.

PETER: Damn! Is she ringing back?

MOLLIE: No. (*PETER's expression changes*) She wanted to know if you could have lunch with her.

PETER: Damn! Damn!

MOLLIE: (*Dead expression; tearing a note off her pad*) I said you could. (*She hands PETER the note*) That's the restaurant. One o'clock.

PETER: (*Delighted*) Mollie, you're a treasure!

MOLLIE: Oh, my God! (*As PETER turns towards his office*) Oh – and Mr Lerner's been trying to get hold of you. He's rung twice already.

PETER: (*Surprised*) Max Lerner?

MOLLIE: Yes.

PETER: Is he in London?

MOLLIE: I think so. It sounded like it.

PETER: Did he say what he wanted?

MOLLIE: No, just that he wanted to talk to you. He's ringing back.

CUT TO: A corner of MAX LERNER's flat. Morning.
MAX looks worried and distinctly tense as he slowly dials a number on his phone.

CUT TO: PETER MATTY's Office. Morning.
PETER is sitting at his desk, dealing with his mail. MOLLIE enters the office with the contract she has been typing.

PETER looks up at her as she puts the document down in front of him.

MOLLIE: Here's the contract for "Design For Loving" – and it reads better than the book.

PETER: Thank you, Mollie. I suppose there hasn't been a call from Scotland?

MOLLIE: Scotland?

PETER: From my brother. He said he'd let me know when he was coming back.

MOLLIE: (*Shaking her head*) No, I'm afraid there hasn't.

The telephone rings. MOLLIE answers it.

MOLLIE: (*On the phone*) Matty Publications …

For the duration of this next conversation, we cut back and forth between PETER's office and MAX's flat.

MAX: This is Max Lerner. Could I speak to Mr Matty, please?

MOLLIE: Just a minute, Mr Lerner. I'll see if he's arrived.

PETER looks at MOLLIE, hesitates, then with a little nod takes the phone from her. MOLLIE goes out.

PETER: (*On the phone; not over friendly*) Good morning, Max. This is a surprise. I thought you'd have gone by now …

MAX: No, I'm … still here. I'd like to see you, Peter. Could we have lunch together?

PETER: Today? I'm sorry. That's not possible.

MAX: Well – could you drop in the flat sometime? This afternoon perhaps, or this evening?

PETER: I'm sorry, Max. I've got a very busy day ahead of me, and this evening …

MAX: (*Stopping PETER*) Look, Peter – this is very important! I've simply got to see you sometime today!

PETER: Important to you – or to me?

MAX: Important to both of us! I'm not trying to borrow money, Peter. It's got nothing to do with money, I assure you!

PETER: Then what is it you want to see me about? (*Pause; MAX doesn't answer*) Hello? …

MAX: I'm still here …

PETER: I said: what is it you want to see me about?

MAX: (*After a moment*) I want to talk to you about … George Delta.

PETER: (*Taken aback*) George Delta?

MAX: Yes.

PETER: Do you know George Delta?

MAX: (*Softly*) Yes, I know him. (*Tensely*) Peter, I've got to see you! Please do as I ask!

PETER: All right, I'll call round this evening. About eight o'clock.

PETER thoughtfully replaces the receiver. A pause – then suddenly he makes a decision and picking up the phone again starts to dial. Half-way through the dialling he hesitates, then changing his mind replaces the receiver.

CUT TO: An Alcove Table in a London Restaurant. Afternoon.

PETER and PHYLLIS have finished lunch and a waiter is offering them more coffee.

WAITER: More coffee, madam?

PHYLLIS shakes her head.

WAITER: Sir?

PETER: No, thank you. (*As the WAITER goes*) Phyllis, you remember the night I came to your hotel – the night we had a drink together?

PHYLLIS: Yes.

PETER: Amongst other things we talked about a man called Max Lerner.

141

PHYLLIS: Did we? I don't remember …

PETER: He's a journalist. He was with me the morning …

PHYLLIS: I remember! He was in the car with you!

PETER: That's right! That's the chap. You said you'd met him.

PHYLLIS: Yes, I met him with my husband, a long time ago.

PETER: Where?

PHYLLIS: In Washington.

PETER: He doesn't remember meeting you.

PHYLLIS: He doesn't? Well – perhaps I'm mistaken. Perhaps I'm thinking of someone else. (*A moment, thoughtfully*) But I don't think I am.

PETER: No, I don't think so either.

PHYLLIS: But why are you interested in this man?

PETER: (*Ignoring the question*) He's done a certain amount of work for me over the years – mostly research work. And he wrote a very good book which we published about five years ago. (*Looking at PHYLLIS*) But tell me what <u>you</u> know about him, Phyllis.

PHYLLIS: (*Puzzled*) I don't know anything about him.

PETER: But you say you met him, in Washington?

PHYLLIS: Yes …

PETER: Where, exactly?

PHYLLIS: Oh, dear! (*A moment; thoughtfully*) I think it was at a party. I seem to remember one of the newspapers gave a party to celebrate something or other and this man Max …?

PETER: Lerner.

PHYLLIS: Was introduced to me.

PETER: By your husband?

PHYLLIS: Yes.

142

PETER: Was he a friend of your husband's?

PHYLLIS: No, I don't think so. In fact, I'm sure he wasn't. (*Puzzled*) But you still haven't answered my question.

PETER: He telephoned me this morning and said he wanted to see me. He said it was important that we met sometime today. When I asked him what he wanted to see me about he said – "George Delta".

PHYLLIS: (*Astonished*) George Delta?

PETER: Yes.

PHYLLIS: Does he know Delta?

PETER: Yes. At least, he says he does.

PHYLLIS: Have you told Osborne about this?

PETER: No, I haven't.

PHYLLIS: You should have done, Peter! I think he ought to know about this phone call. I really do.

PETER: I was going to telephone him, in fact I started to do so, then at the very last moment I changed my mind.

PHYLLIS: Why?

PETER: I thought perhaps I ought to see Max first and listen to what he's got to say. Perhaps I was wrong. I don't know. Anyway, I'll phone Osborne tonight.

PHYLLIS: When are you seeing this man?

PETER: This evening.

PHYLLIS: Perhaps we could meet later, after you've seen him? I'd like to know what happens.

PETER: Yes, of course. I'll meet you here … No, wait a minute! That's not a very good idea. (*Thoughtfully*) I'm seeing him at eight o'clock but I'm not sure how long I'll be with him.

> Perhaps it would be better if you came to my flat?

PHYLLIS: Yes, all right.

PETER: I'll give you a key and you can let yourself in, in case you get there first. (*He takes out his wallet and produces a card*) Here's the address, it's very easy to find.

PHYLLIS: (*Taking the card*) Thank you. (*A moment, then:*) And take care, Peter.

CUT TO: A Street in Islington. Night.
This street is just around the corner from MAX LERNER's flat. PETER is busy parking his car in a vacant space. Eventually satisfied with the car's position he climbs out of the Jaguar and starts to lock the car doors.

CUT TO: The entrance of a block of flats. Night.
PETER enters the building and crosses to the entry-phone on the wall. He presses the "MAX LERNER" button and stands waiting for a reply. He presses the button again; there is still no reply. PETER hesitates and is about to press the button for a third time when a man's voice is heard over the entry-phone.

MAN: Hello …

PETER: It's Peter, Max. I'm coming up.

CUT TO: First Floor Corridor. Night.
PETER arrives in the corridor and crosses to MAX LERNER's front door. He stops dead, staring at the door in obvious surprise. There is a Yale key in the lock. PETER hesitates, not quite sure what to do, then turning the key he gently pushes the door open.

CUT TO: The Hall of MAX LERNER's Flat. Night.

As the door gradually opens, we see the dead body of MAX LERNER spreadeagled across the hall carpet. PETER is staggered; he stares at the body in dazed amazement. It is several seconds before he finally decides to enter the hall. He moves slowly, hesitatingly, towards the body. He is kneeling by MAX, briefly examining him, when the living room door opens. CLAUDE is standing in the doorway. He is wearing a light overcoat and a pair of gloves. There is a tense moment as he stares at PETER. Then he slowly raises his right hand. It is then that PETER sees the gun CLAUDE is holding.

CUT TO: New Scotland Yard. Night.

A police car is waiting outside of the side building. Two uniformed men are in the car and a plain-clothes officer – DETECTIVE INSPECTOR HOLROYD – is standing by the open car door obviously waiting for someone. After a moment OSBORNE rushes out of the building and with a brief nod to HOLROYD climbs into the car. He is quickly followed by the INSPECTOR. The car takes off, lights flashing, sirens screeching.

CUT TO: The Hall of MAX LERNER's Flat. Night.

PETER is still kneeling by the body of MAX LERNER, but he is staring at the gun in CLAUDE's hand. He slowly rises and as he does so CLAUDE lowers the gun.

PETER: He's dead …
CLAUDE: Yes, I know.
PETER: Claude, what the hell are you doing here?
CLAUDE: I'll explain later.
PETER: (*Angry*) Explain now!
CLAUDE: (*Shaking his head*) I'll explain later when Osborne gets here.

145

PETER: (*Surprised*) Osborne! You've sent for the police?

CLAUDE: Yes, of course! Of course, I have! Good God, Peter, surely you don't think I had anything to do with this! You don't think I killed him!

As PETER stares at CLAUDE, not sure whether to believe him or not, we suddenly hear the sound of the approaching police car.

CUT TO: The Living Room of MAX LERNER's Flat. Night.

PETER and CLAUDE are being questioned by OSBORNE and INSPECTOR HOLROYD. There is obvious police activity in the hall at the rear of the living room although the body has been removed.

OSBORNE: (*To PETER*) You say you had an appointment with Mr Lerner?

PETER: Yes.

OSBORNE: Did he make the appointment, sir?

PETER: Yes, he did.

OSBORNE: When?

PETER: This morning, he telephoned my office. He said he wanted to see me and that the matter was urgent. I arranged to see him here, at eight o'clock.

HOLROYD: What was it he wanted to see you about? Have you any idea?

PETER: Yes, I have. (*He looks at OSBORNE*) It was about a man called George Delta.

OSBORNE: George Delta!

PETER: Yes.

CLAUDE: (*Slowly*) Are you sure he said that? That he wanted to talk to you about George Delta?

PETER: Yes, I'm quite sure.

146

OSBORNE: (*To CLAUDE*) You seem surprised, sir?

CLAUDE: I am surprised. Very surprised. And for a very good reason. You see, I happen to know that Max Lerner and George Delta were, in fact, one and the same person.

A slight pause.

OSBORNE and PETER are staring at CLAUDE.

OSBORNE: (*To CLAUDE; quietly*) Go on, Mr Matty. Tell us what else you know.

CLAUDE: Well – I think perhaps I'd better start by telling you what happened to an Italian conductor; Enrico Muralto. About three weeks ago he committed suicide in Madrid. His wife, Eva, was a great friend of mine and like everyone else she was deeply distressed and mystified by her husband's death. Although at the time, I must admit, there were rumours – very strong rumours – that Enrico was being blackmailed. After her husband's death I stayed with Eva for two or three days, helping her to sort out various documents. During the course of this we came across a photograph. The photograph puzzled Eva because she'd never seen it before and, apart from Enrico, the people in the snapshot were completely unknown to her.

A slight pause.

OSBORNE: (*Quietly*) Go on, Mr Matty.

CLAUDE: Three days ago I suddenly decided I'd like to take another look at that photograph, so I contacted Eva, and flew to Rome.

PETER: (*Surprised*) Rome?

CLAUDE: Yes, Peter. (*To OSBORNE*) I arrived back this evening. The first thing I did was telephone this number (*He indicates the phone*) and talk to Max Lerner.

CUT TO: An Open Telephone Booth, London Airport. Night.

CLAUDE is standing under the plastic cover, dialling a number.

CUT TO: The Living Room of MAX LERNER's Flat. Night.

The telephone is ringing, and MAX comes out of the bathroom, an electric razor in his hand. He puts the razor down as he picks up the phone. For the duration of this conversation, we cut back and forth between MAX and CLAUDE.

MAX: 226-7081 …
CLAUDE: Max Lerner?
MAX: Yes – speaking …
CLAUDE: This is Claude Matty, Mr Lerner. I understand you're a friend of my brother's?
MAX: (*Curious*) Yes, that's right, Mr Matty.
CLAUDE: I'm at London Airport at the moment; I've just arrived. I'd like to see you. Will you be in this evening?
MAX: (*Puzzled*) Yes, as a matter of fact I'm seeing your brother at eight o'clock. But – why do you wish to see me, Mr Matty?
CLAUDE: (*Quietly*) Can't you guess why?
MAX: No, I'm afraid I can't.
CLAUDE: Oh, forgive me. I didn't tell you where I'd been. (*Significantly*) I've been to Rome, to see Mrs Muralto.
MAX: (*A moment, then:*) Mrs – Muralto?
CLAUDE: That's right.

148

MAX:	I'm – I'm sorry, but that doesn't mean anything to me. I don't know anyone of that name.
CLAUDE:	Don't you? That does surprise me! It surprises me very much because I have a photograph of you with Mrs Muralto's husband – Enrico.

A tiny pause.

MAX:	Where did you get this photograph?
CLAUDE:	Let's just say we found it, Mrs Muralto and I …

Another pause.

MAX:	(*Quietly*) What is it you want?
CLAUDE:	I want to talk to you, that's all. Believe me, I'm not trying to play your game. I'm not trying to blackmail you, if that's what you're thinking.

Another pause.

MAX:	(*A note of weariness in his voice*) I – I didn't blackmail Enrico.
CLAUDE:	Then what did you do?
MAX:	I found out things about him and passed the information on. But I didn't blackmail him! I swear I didn't!
CLAUDE:	It's a distinction I'd like to discuss with you. I have an excellent bottle of brandy with me. Duty free. What do you say, Mr Lerner?
MAX:	(*Fatalistically*) All right. All right, if you must. I was going to talk to your brother anyway. I'll be here all evening.

MAX slowly replaces the receiver.

149

CUT TO: The Living Room of MAX LERNER's Flat.
               Night.

OSBORNE, INSPECTOR HOLROYD, and PETER are listening to CLAUDE.

CLAUDE: … I arrived here at about ten minutes to eight. I tried the entry-phone in the lobby, but nothing happened, so after a little while I came upstairs. The front door was closed, and I couldn't get any reply. I hung around for about five minutes not quite sure what to do, then just as I was turning away, I noticed that someone had pushed a key under the door. I picked it up and let myself into the flat. The rest you know. I found Lerner and telephoned Scotland Yard. Five minutes later my brother arrived.

HOLROYD is looking at CLAUDE, not quite sure what to make of his story.

HOLROYD: I see. Thank you. (*He glances at OSBORNE*)
PETER: (*To CLAUDE*) So it was you that I spoke to? (*Indicating the wall entry-phone*)
CLAUDE: Yes, it was.
HOLROYD: And the gun, Mr Matty? Where did you say you found it?
CLAUDE: I told you, I found it on the floor, near the chair. It was either left there deliberately or … someone dropped it.
HOLROYD: Is that so? That's interesting.
CLAUDE: Well – er – that's only my opinion, of course.
OSBORNE: You should have left it where it was, sir. But since you didn't, I'm glad you had the sense to put your gloves on …
HOLROYD: Yes. It was lucky you had them with you.

PETER looks at HOLROYD.

150

CLAUDE: I suppose it was. But I frequently wear
               gloves. I … have to take care of my hands.

*CLAUDE glances at PETER who, somewhat puzzled by his
brother's manner, is staring at him with a faint suggestion of
suspicion.*

HOLROYD: Yes, well – you'll have to come down to the
               Station, sir. We shall want to take your
               fingerprints …

CLAUDE: Yes, of course. I realise that.

HOLROYD: (*To PETER*) You too, sir.

PETER: (*To OSBORNE; after a slight hesitation*) I
               have an appointment later this evening with
               Mrs Du Salle. I'd very much like to keep it if
               possible.

OSBORNE makes no comment, simply gives a little nod.

HOLROYD: (*To CLAUDE*) When you entered the flat did
               you see anything or hear anything which
               aroused your curiosity – apart from the dead
               man?

CLAUDE: Yes, I heard what I thought was a door
               closing and I rushed through into the kitchen.
               The back door was shut but I immediately
               looked outside to see if I could see anyone.

HOLROYD: And did you see anyone?

CLAUDE: No, I didn't. But I don't think I was mistaken.
               You see, there's a brass chain on the door and
               when I entered the kitchen it was moving
               slightly.

HOLROYD: Very observant of you, Mr Matty.

CLAUDE: (*Resenting the remark*) I don't think so. It was
               pretty noticeable.

HOLROYD: You say you arrived at London Airport this
               evening?

151

CLAUDE: Yes. I was on the British Airways flight from Rome. We landed at 6.15.

HOLROYD: And the first thing you did was telephone Mr Lerner.

CLAUDE: That's right.

HOLROYD: What happened after you spoke to Mr Lerner?

CLAUDE: I told you! I jumped in a cab and came straight here.

HOLROYD: You didn't telephone anyone else?

CLAUDE: No.

OSBORNE: Not even your brother?

PETER looks at OSBORNE.

CLAUDE: No.

OSBORNE: Why not? I would have thought that was the obvious thing to have done.

CLAUDE: It was then a quarter to seven. I knew if Peter kept his appointment, I'd be seeing him at eight o'clock anyway, so … Besides, I wanted to see Lerner first. I wanted to question him about the photograph.

CLAUDE takes a photograph out of his pocket, looks at it for a moment, then slowly hands it over to OSBORNE.

CUT TO: The Living Room of PETER's Flat. Night.
PETER is sitting in an armchair, deep in thought. He has changed his jacket for a dressing-gown and there is a drink on the coffee table by the side of his chair. Background music is coming from a radio and at the same time the front doorbell is ringing. The bell continues ringing for some little time, but PETER appears to be oblivious to it. Finally, there is the sound of the front door opening and closing. PETER suddenly becomes aware of this and jumping out of the chair moves towards the hall.

PHYLLIS: (*In the hall*) Peter!

PETER: Phyllis! Come in, my dear!

PHYLLIS enters from the hall.

PHYLLIS: I wasn't sure you were here.

PETER: (*Indicating the armchair*) I'm sorry, I was miles away. I heard the bell, and I just didn't realise it was the front door.

PETER crosses and switches off the radio. PHYLLIS watches him, aware that he is somewhat tense and on edge.

PHYLLIS: What is it, Peter? You look terribly worried. Has something happened?

PETER: Yes, but – first let me get you a drink.

PHYLLIS: No, no, I don't want a drink! Tell me – why are you looking so worried? What happened tonight?

PETER takes PHYLLIS's coat before answering.

PETER: (*Quietly*) Max Lerner's dead. He was murdered.

PHYLLIS: (*Stunned*) When?

PETER: Tonight. Just before I arrived at his flat.

PHYLLIS: You mean – he was actually dead when you got there?

PETER: Yes. His body was in the hall. He'd been shot.

PHYLLIS: This is terrible! My God, what a shock it must have been! Have the police any idea who did it?

PETER: (*On edge*) I don't know, Phyllis. It's difficult to say …

PHYLLIS: (*A sudden thought*) They surely don't think that you had anything to do with it?

PETER: (*Tensely*) I don't know … (*Shaking his head*) No, I don't think so, but … My brother was there. He was in the flat when I arrived. Apparently, he telephoned Max earlier this evening and arranged to see him. At least, that's what he says.

PHYLLIS looks at PETER, surprised by the doubt in his voice.

153

PHYLLIS:	That's what he says? Does that mean you don't believe him?
PETER:	I don't know whether to believe him or not! He told the police such an extraordinary story. I find it difficult to … I just don't know what to believe, Phyllis!

A slight pause.

PHYLLIS:	Was your brother a friend of Max Lerner's?
PETER:	No.
PHYLLIS:	Then why did he want to see him?
PETER:	It's a good question. And it's one I've been asking myself all evening. Three days ago, Claude told me he was going up to Scotland on business. It now transpires that he didn't go to Scotland, he went to Rome instead. He went to see a friend of his – a Mrs Muralto.
PHYLLIS:	Mrs Muralto?
PETER:	Yes. Have you heard the name before?
PHYLLIS:	(*Thoughtfully*) Yes, I think I have. Her husband was a conductor. He committed suicide …
PETER:	That's right.

The doorbell is ringing.

PHYLLIS:	I remember reading about it. It happened in Madrid.
PETER:	Well, apparently Claude … (*He stops; looks towards the hall*)
PHYLLIS:	Are you expecting anyone?
PETER:	(*Puzzled; shaking his head*) No. Excuse me.

PETER hesitates, then goes out into the hall. PHYLLIS moves towards the hall, obviously curious. We hear the opening of the front door.

OSBORNE:	(*Off*) Sorry to disturb you, Mr Matty, but – I'd very much like to have a word with you, if possible?
PETER:	(*Off; surprised*) Yes, of course! Come along in.
OSBORNE:	(*Off*) Thank you.

The front door closes.

PETER:	(*Off*) Mrs Du Salle is here …
OSBORNE:	(*Off*) Oh, I'm sorry, if I'd known I wouldn't have troubled you. I'd have telephoned.
PETER:	(*Off*) That's all right, go ahead!

OSBORNE enters with PETER.

OSBORNE:	Good evening, Mrs Du Salle.
PHYLLIS:	Good evening.
OSBORNE:	(*To PETER*) I'm awfully sorry to disturb you like this, but it is important.
PHYLLIS:	(*A shade embarrassed*) Would you like me to …
OSBORNE:	No, no, please! Don't go! I'm sure Mr Matty's told you about this evening?
PHYLLIS:	About Mr Lerner? Yes, he has.
PETER:	We were just talking about it.
PHYLLIS:	Have you any idea who … was responsible?
OSBORNE:	No, we haven't – not yet. But there's been a rather curious development. (*To PETER*) Mr Matty, tell me; when you spoke to Mr Lerner – this morning, on the telephone – did you say quite definitely that you would be seeing him this evening?
PETER:	Yes, I did.
OSBORNE:	You left no doubt in his mind?
PETER:	(*Thoughtfully*) No, I don't think so … I'm pretty sure I said I'd drop in about eight o'clock. But why do you ask?

OSBORNE: (*A slight pause*) It would appear that Mr Lerner was under the impression that you might not 'drop in'. So, he wrote you a letter.

PETER: A letter?

OSBORNE: Yes. The letter was registered and sent to this address. It was posted this morning, shortly after he spoke to you on the phone. (*He takes a slip of paper from his pocket*) We found the receipt.

PETER: But – what's in the letter?

OSBORNE: Your guess is as good as mine. But I shall be surprised, very surprised, if it doesn't contain some interesting information. (*With authority*) Anyway, the important thing is this. Don't open the letter, Mr Matty. Get in touch with me the moment it arrives. You understand?

CUT TO: A London Street. Morning.

There are several cars parked in this side street, including a Mini. A POSTMAN is strolling down the street carrying the morning mail.

CUT TO: The Living Room of PETER's Flat. Morning.

The telephone is ringing. PETER comes out of the bedroom, holding a book he has been reading, and crosses to the phone. PETER puts down the book and picks up the receiver.

PETER: Hello … Peter Matty …

There is no intercutting in this scene. We simply hear OSBORNE's voice on the other end of the line.

OSBORNE: Good morning, Mr Matty. Osborne here …

PETER: I'm sorry. The post hasn't arrived yet.

OSBORNE: I know it hasn't. Not to worry. It will. (*A moment, then:*) Is your brother with you?

PETER: No, he went out about half an hour ago.

156

OSBORNE:	Will he be coming back?
PETER:	(*Puzzled*) Not for some little time.
OSBORNE:	I see. (*Tiny pause*) Are you alone?
PETER:	Yes.
OSBORNE:	Then please, get a chair and sit down. I want to talk to you.
PETER:	(*Curious*) That's all right. Go ahead …
OSBORNE:	(*Quietly*) Get the chair, Mr Matty. I think you're going to need it.

CUT TO: A luxury block of flats. London.

The POSTMAN can be seen in the distance walking down the road towards the block of flats. He stops to have a friendly word with a passer-by, finally continuing his journey and entering the building.

CUT TO: The Living Room of PETER's Flat. Morning.

PETER is still on the phone, listening to OSBORNE. He looks both tense and worried. As before we only hear OSBORNE's voice.

OSBORNE:	… That's it, I'm afraid. It's not the whole story, but I'll fill in the details later.
PETER:	(*Quietly*) Thank you.
OSBORNE:	I knew it would be a shock, Mr Matty, and I'm sorry I had to break it to you like this.
PETER:	(*Tonelessly*) That's all right.
OSBORNE:	Believe me, I really had no alternative.

The doorbell is ringing.

| PETER: | I understand. Thank you for putting me in the picture. |

PETER slowly replaces the receiver and stands deep in thought, almost dazed by the information he has received from OSBORNE. The doorbell continues to ring. After a long pause, he turns towards the hall.

157

CUT TO: The Hall of PETER's Flat. Morning.

The front doorbell is still ringing as PETER comes out of the living room and, crossing the hall, opens the front door.

POSTMAN: Morning, sir. Registered letter. (*As PETER takes the letter and signs for it*) Just the one. No bills this morning.

PETER gives a little nod and closes the door.

CUT TO: The Living Room of PETER's Flat. Morning.

Peter enters the living room with the registered letter in his hand and walks slowly down towards the coffee table and his favourite armchair. He sits on the arm of the chair, staring at the letter, but making no attempt to open it. After a little while, he puts the envelope down on the coffee table and glances at his watch. Although there is still an unmistakable air of despondency about him there is now a suggestion of alertness; tenseness even. He is looking at his watch for the second time when he hears a noise in the hall. The sound of a key in the front door.

A pause.

PHYLLIS appears. She has a gun in her hand.

PETER: (*In as ordinary a voice as he can manage*) Hello, Phyllis. I've been expecting you.

PHYLLIS faces PETER, defiantly.

PHYLLIS: Give me the letter!

PETER: You shall have it. All in good time. (*He picks up the letter*) But first, we talk!

PHYLLIS: (*Quietly, but with a threatening undertone*) I didn't come here to talk. Give me the letter!

PETER: What happened the night your husband disappeared? Did he find out about you? Did he find out that you'd been blackmailing his friends? Or were you both in it together and was it simply a case of ...

158

PHYLLIS: (*Stopping PETER*) You saw what happened to
               Lerner! Give me the letter!

A slight pause.

PETER: Claude recognised you. That's why he went to
               Rome.

PHYLLIS: I know that!

PETER: He'd seen a photograph of you with Enrico and
               Max Lerner.

*PETER suddenly backs away from PHYLLIS; for a second or
two it looks as if she is about to shoot him.*

PHYLLIS: Don't you think I'm serious? Don't you think
               I'll use this?

Another pause.

PETER is looking at PHYLLIS.

PETER: After what happened to Max and Mrs
               Braithwaite, I'm quite sure you'll use it,
               Phyllis.

PHYLLIS: (*Quietly*) Then give me the letter.

*A moment – then PETER hands PHYLLIS the letter. She puts
it under her arm.*

PHYLLIS: Here's your door key.

*PHYLLIS holds out the key and as PETER reaches for it the
key 'accidentally' slips through PHYLLIS's fingers. PETER
stoops to retrieve it from the carpet and as he does so
PHYLLIS brings the gun crashing down on his head. As soon
as she is convinced that PETER is unconscious, PHYLLIS
crosses to the telephone and rips it away from its socket –
then she turns, and, after a quick glance at PETER rushes out
into the hall.*

CUT TO: The Block of Flats. Morning.

*PHYLLIS emerges from the block of flats and hurries towards
the end of the road.*

CUT TO: A London Street. Morning.
PHYLLIS reaches the Mini, unlocks the door of the car, and gets into the driving seat.

CUT TO: Inside the Mini. Morning.
PHYLLIS is at the driving wheel. She is looking at the registered letter, trying to make up her mind whether to open it now or wait until later. Suddenly she makes a decision and tearing open the envelope takes out the letter. She stares in amazement at the contents. The notepaper in the envelope is blank. There is no letter from MAX LERNER. PHYLLIS quickly realises that she has fallen for a trap of some kind. She drops the letter and immediately starts the car.

CUT TO: A London Street. Morning.
The Mini pulls away from the kerb and races down the street towards a main road. As it reaches the corner a police car turns into the street and brakes to a standstill, deliberately barring the Mini's exit into the main road.

CUT TO: Inside the Mini. Morning.
PHYLLIS is staring through the windscreen at the police car. She sees two uniformed men get out of the car followed by INSPECTOR HOLROYD. PHYLLIS makes another quick decision and puts the Mini into reverse.

CUT TO: A London Street. Morning.
As the Mini, in reverse, gathers speed a second police car arrives on the scene, entering the street from the opposite end.

CUT TO: Inside the Mini. Morning.
PHYLLIS sees the second car through the rear window of the Mini and realises that there is now no way of escape. She gradually brings the car to a standstill.

160

CUT TO: A London Street. Morning.
The second police car stops some little distance away from the Mini and OSBORNE gets out of this car and walks slowly towards PHYLLIS.

CUT TO: Inside the Mini. Morning.
PHYLLIS is now holding the gun in her hand. She looks grimly determined as OSBORNE slowly approaches the Mini. There is a pause, then PHYLLIS raises the gun as if to fire at the approaching figure of OSBORNE – instead she slowly puts the revolver to her head.

CUT TO: A London Street. Morning.
OSBORNE suddenly realises what PHYLLIS is doing and with a cry rushes towards the Mini. He is too late. Before he reaches the car there is the sound of a shot. OSBORNE stops in his tracks, a look of horror on his face.

CUT TO: Poole Harbour. Afternoon.
CLAUDE is sitting on a stone pillar near the water's edge, obviously waiting for someone. A police car appears at the entrance to the marina and as CLAUDE rises to his feet OSBORNE can be seen getting out of the car.

CUT TO: The Entrance to Poole Harbour. Afternoon.
OSBORNE is talking to the uniformed driver of the car.
OSBORNE: Thank you. Pick me up in about an hour.
The driver nods and commences to turn the car round. OSBORNE sees CLAUDE approaching and walks towards him. The two men shake hands on meeting.
OSBORNE: (*Friendly*) Hello, Mr Matty! Nice to see you.
CLAUDE: It's good of you to come down.
OSBORNE: Not at all. You look well, I must say. How's your brother?

CLAUDE: Physically he's completely recovered, of
             course, but – well, I suppose no man likes to
             think he's been made a fool of.

*CLAUDE and OSBORNE have started strolling along the
quay towards PETER's boat.*

OSBORNE: You don't have to tell me that! I'm afraid I
             haven't exactly come out of this affair with
             flying colours!

CLAUDE: Oh – I wouldn't say that.

OSBORNE: I would! Unlike my colleague, Mrs
             Braithwaite, I was taken in by Phyllis Du
             Salle. Utterly and completely. In fact, if you
             hadn't recognised her, God knows what
             would have happened.

CLAUDE: Well – at the time, I must confess, I wasn't a
             hundred per cent sure.

OSBORNE: I'm more than grateful for the help you gave
             us. We all are. Incidentally, you'll be
             interested to know I've had several
             conversations with my opposite number in
             Marseilles. He tells me they never completely
             believed Phyllis Du Salle's story. It's true her
             husband collected dolls of various
             nationalities – it was his hobby – but the
             French have always suspected that their row
             was about something quite different.

CLAUDE: You mean Phyllis invented the story about the
             doll being in the bathroom in order to
             substantiate her statement and divert
             suspicion from herself?

OSBORNE: Yes, and she used the same technique over
             here. She planted a doll in your brother's flat
             immediately after Mrs Braithwaite was

162

murdered. It's what the Americans call 'a bum steer'.

CLAUDE: How do you know she planted the doll?

OSBORNE: I'd like to tell you it was a case of simple deduction on my part. But, alas, it wouldn't be true. Mortimer Brown told me.

CLAUDE: (*Surprised*) Mortimer Brown?

OSBORNE: (*Nodding*) We picked up Mr Brown yesterday afternoon, in Belfast.

CLAUDE: And he talked?

OSBORNE: Yes. (*With a smile; quite simply*) He didn't have much choice, Mr Matty. We're charging him with the Cassidy murder. I only hope it sticks.

CUT TO: The Cabin of First Edition. Afternoon.

PETER, CLAUDE, and OSBORNE are sitting around the table. PETER looks tired and a shade depressed but he is listening to what OSBORNE is saying with obvious interest.

OSBORNE: … After Phyllis got rid of her husband, she took complete control of the organisation. She'd been working with him for some time, of course, and she knew most of their contacts. By 'contacts' I mean people who supplied them with information and photographs.

PETER: People like Max Lerner and Mortimer Brown?

OSBORNE: Yes, and Sir Arnold Wyatt's son-in-law. Incidentally, I don't know whether you realise it or not, Mr Matty, but she was hoping to find out something about you.

PETER: About me?

OSBORNE: Yes, that's why your flat was searched.

163

CLAUDE: But tell me: why was the photograph of Phyllis in Mortimer Brown's window?

OSBORNE: Phyllis had never met Brown and she wanted to make quite sure that he was willing to cooperate with her. Her husband had had trouble with him in the past and she wasn't even sure whether he was prepared to meet her or not. The photograph signified that he was. As soon as Phyllis saw it, she telephoned for an appointment.

CLAUDE: And Brown simply replaced her photograph with the one that had been in the window originally?

OSBORNE: That's right. Unfortunately, Mrs Cassidy was in the shop when Phyllis telephoned, and she overheard part of the conversation. She made up her mind to tell you about it. Brown warned her not to, but she took no notice of him and got in touch with you. (*A shrug*) The rest you know.

PETER: I'm sorry Max was mixed up in all this. I know, strictly speaking, he was no damn good, but – well, in a curious sort of way we were quite fond of each other.

OSBORNE: He got out of his depth, I'm afraid. That was Mr Lerner's trouble.

PETER: Why do you think he wanted to see me, the night he was murdered?

OSBORNE: I think he was about to leave the country and was prepared to tell you the whole story. For a price, Mr Matty.

PETER: (*Thoughtfully*) Yes. Yes, knowing Max, you could be right. (*He rises*) Well, I don't know about you gentlemen, but I need a drink!

PETER *crosses to the bottles on the sideboard.*

OSBORNE: If you'll forgive my saying so, sir, I think what you really need is a holiday.

CLAUDE: I couldn't agree more! (*To OSBORNE*) I'm giving a recital in Monte Carlo at the end of the month and I'm having a devil of a job trying to persuade him to come out with me.

OSBORNE: I wish someone would try and talk me into going to Monte Carlo!

PETER *turns, smiles at OSBORNE, and picks up a bottle of whisky.*

PETER: Scotch?

CUT TO: London Airport. Day.

A Ford Zephyr (Private Hire) draws up at the kerb and CLAUDE gets out followed by PETER. As CLAUDE pays the driver a porter arrives on the scene and, helped by PETER, collects the baggage and loads it onto a trolley.

Whilst this is happening a taxi pulls up immediately behind the Ford and an extremely pretty girl emerges from it. PETER notices her. The girl is carrying a passport wallet, a travel case, a small bouquet of flowers, and several magazines. Her arms are indeed full. As she turns towards the cab driver the wallet very nearly slips through her fingers and in a desperate attempt to retrieve it, she drops both the bouquet and several of her magazines. PETER sees what is happening and immediately goes to her aid. He is smiling at the girl and helping her to collect her things when he suddenly feels a warning hand on his shoulder. Looking up, he sees CLAUDE. CLAUDE takes the bouquet out of his brother's hand, presents it to the somewhat bewildered girl, then leads PETER gently but firmly into the airport building.

165

THE END

Printed in Great Britain
by Amazon

57054676R00108